Jack London

TWELVE SHORT STORIES

Jack London

TWELVE SHORT STORIES

edited by JEFFERY TILLETT

Bramcote Hills Technical Grammar School, Nottingham

Illustrated by
DAVID BARLOW

Edward Arnold

© Jeffery Tillett 1969

First published 1969
by Edward Arnold (Publishers) Ltd
25 Hill Street
London W1X 8LL

Reprinted 1972

ISBN: 0 7131 1557 2

Printed in Great Britain by
Western Printing Services Ltd, Bristol

Contents

Introduction

Jack London, Son of the Wild

A young boy stands in the entrance of the Oakland Public Library. Untidy, unkempt, with an uncared-for look about him, he is clearly a boy from the San Francisco dockland. As he stands there, small yet stocky for his ten years, and nervously twisting his cap in his hand, his eyes fill with wonder: he never believed that there could be so many books in the world as those he saw before him. He had never known before that there was such a thing as a public library where books were available free and for the asking. In the five years that he had been reading, the only books he had read, apart from those at school, had been discarded dime novels or old newspapers though he had known of course that, somewhere, real books with beautiful covers and pictures, some even in colour, must exist. He felt now that he had not a minute to waste; he would read them all. He certainly lost no time in getting hold of all the adventure stories, and especially books about the sea and foreign travel, about discoveries and achievement, that he could lay his hands on. Not one moment of the day was to be wasted; he read at home, at table, in bed, in playtime breaks at school when others were playing, and even as he walked to and from school. And when he grew up he too would have a large house piled high with bookshelves, every one of them filled to overflowing. One day that dream was to come true, for the nervous boy who stood at the door of the Library that day in Oakland

7

was Jack London and, in later years, he was to look back on that day as the most important one in his life for it was on that day that he was re-born in the sense that it saw the emergence into the world of his spirit.

Jack London had been born in San Francisco on 12th January, 1876. His father, John London, was a widower whose first wife had died after bearing him ten children, the two youngest of whom, both girls, he took with him to his second family home. John London was a farmer of English ancestry, he was a skilful farmer too and at first all went well. But, unfortunately, he was no businessman and put his trust in too many people who later let him down. Then too his second wife, young Jack's mother, was quite unpredictable and a poor manager of the household resources. As a result, the family was brought up against a background of economic insecurity; they never quite managed to make ends meet. The children, especially Jack, were often left to their own devices and young Jack early became acquainted with the seamy side of San Francisco dock-life, its bars, its wharves, its riff-raff and dregs of humanity. But this experience was later to be invaluable to him as a writer; let loose, he observed humanity in all its variety and stored his impressions to be put to good use later on. Many of his social novels and several of his short stories recall these early formative years and draw on the memories he retained of them.

Then real tragedy struck the family. After a succession of jobs, John London found work as a night-watchman on the San Francisco wharves. One night, an accident on duty incapacitated him; he was now a permanent invalid. Thus at the age of fourteen young Jack London found himself the breadwinner of the family, his stepsister Eliza having by now herself married and taken her younger sister to live with her.

While at school, Jack had already taken on a variety of odd jobs to help supplement the family income. (His youthful energies had not been wholly dissipated and wasted.) He had worked in a bowling alley and sold newspapers in the streets. He had helped the fishermen in the Bay. Indeed, by the age of thirteen he had acquired his own little boat and had earned for himself quite a reputation as a budding young sailor. But now he was faced with the prospect of full-time work and this time in deadly earnest, not partly for the fun of it. His first real job was in a canning factory: deadly monotonous, soul-destroying work, especially for one of young Jack's disposition. He liked the outdoor life; a life of activity, adventure and enterprise.

Working ten to sixteen hours a day in a factory for a few dollars a week was not his idea of earning a living. Something of the frustration he suffered at this time is conveyed to us in *The Apostate*, one of the stories included in this collection.

Now there were at this time operating in the San Francisco Bay several gangs of 'oyster-pirates' who, under cover of darkness, went out and raided the oyster beds and sold their illegally-gotten gains in the city by day. Jack threw up his job at the factory and joined one of these gangs. He was soon earning in one single raid as much as he had earned from two or three weeks' work in the canning factory. Soon he became more ambitious. With money borrowed from his old coloured nurse he bought his own sloop, *The Razzle Dazzle*. At fifteen years of age he was his own master.

For two years he led this wild and dangerous life. When he was not raiding the oyster beds in the Bay, he was drinking on land, well on the way to becoming an inveterate alcoholic. In later years he was to recall these wild days in *Martin Eden* and *John Barleycorn*, both of which are partly autobiographical and are partly centred on the San Francisco water front.

Then quite suddenly he changed sides. From being an out-law he became a lawman—he joined the State Fish Patrol whose job it was to pursue and arrest illegal fishermen! This was a job he took up with a vast store of experience—from the other side. To his adventures at this period of his life we owe two books, *The Cruise of the Dazzler* and *Tales of the Fish Patrol*, both written (specially for young people) just after he had made his reputation as a writer with *The Call of the Wild*. Then at the age of seventeen he sailed on a sealing vessel bound for the Pacific; on it he spent seven strenuous but happy months, including a visit to Japan.

He returned to his home in Oakland, San Francisco, in the late summer of 1893. At this time America was in the throes of a serious economic crisis. Millions were out of work, and Jack London found himself one of them. To this period belongs his conversion to Socialism. He took to the road for a time as a tramp and travelled rough for thousands of miles over the United States, often as a train stowaway. He underwent all manner of hardships and privations, and he even received a short prison sentence in a Penitentiary for vagrancy. Shortly after this he was taking part in an organized march of the un-employed which aimed to converge on Washington. (There is nothing new about the protest marches and political demon-strations we read about today.) The march failed and Jack

London was one of those who found himself in a prison cell, this time as a political agitator.

It would not be true to assume that up to this point in his life London had spent his time entirely in rough, tough—and often illegal—physical activity. Afloat and ashore he was still an omnivorous reader. He was not particularly selective in what he read; he took up whatever interested and fascinated him at any particular time. One of the chief criticisms levelled against London as a writer is the very uneven quality of his writing. Perhaps this is due to his own inability to be selective as a reader; though as we shall see, there were other reasons too.

His favourite authors among writers of fiction were Rudyard Kipling especially his stories set in the then British-ruled India; Robert Louis Stevenson, author of *Treasure Island*, *Kidnapped*, and *Dr. Jekyll and Mr. Hyde*, who lived his last days in Samoa in the Pacific where he was known as *Tusitala* (the teller of tales); and Joseph Conrad, the Polish seaman who became a naturalized British subject and one of Britain's greatest writers of stories of the sea. The influence of all three, and of Herman Melville, author of *Moby Dick*, can be seen in his early works, particularly their zest for life and manly adventure.

His reading was by no means confined to works of fiction. The world in which Jack London grew up was, intellectually, a fascinating one. In England Charles Darwin had set out his theories on evolution in *The Origin of Species* (1859) and *The Descent of Man* (1871). In the field of politics Karl Marx had published the Communist Manifesto (1848) and, as a political refugee in London, *Das Kapital* (1867), translated into English in 1886. In Europe Frederick Nietzsche, a German, had used the term 'superman' to describe a new race which would emerge, superior because the weaklings had disappeared from it. His writings were much misunderstood; many who had never read a word of his scholarly works seized upon this one word 'superman' to justify theories of 'Master race' and policies of euthanasia and genocide, systematically killing of the weaker members of society (as the Nazis did) to achieve more quickly the sort of world that Nietzsche foresaw. In England Herbert Spencer had said more or less the same thing from a philosophical point of view and used these views to justify poverty, unemployment and other social miseries. John Stuart Mill with his theories of 'Utilitarianism' and 'laissez-faire' (i.e. leave things alone to work out their own solution) shared these ideas, though from an economic viewpoint. All these theories, their authors and their books were known to Jack

London. Although they were in many respects, particularly Marx and Nietzsche, diametrically opposed, he read them impartially and took over many of their contradictory ideas both in his writings and in his attitude to life.

Thus it was that in 1895 he made another important decision. He decided to remedy his hitherto chequered education and return home to Oakland to sign on at High School. Here he established himself as a writer of no mean ability.

The school magazine gave him the opportunity of seeing his work in print. He took a prominent part in the affairs of the debating society, and continued his political activities, which soon again landed him in jail, this time for speaking in a public park without a licence.

At the age of 20, London passed the entrance examination which qualified him to enter the University of California. Unfortunately his father's worsening state of health obliged him to give up his studies after one year, and to return home to Oakland to support the family.

Once more it was back to heavy manual labour for Jack London. But this time with a difference, for he had now an added interest in life—his writing. Short stories, articles, poetry poured from his pen, but he failed to find a publisher. Time and again his manuscripts were returned to him. At last, thoroughly frustrated, he packed his belongings—including books and notepaper—and set off North to the Klondyke to join in the great American Gold Rush. It was then March 1897, and London was just turned 21.

Twelve months later he returned. He brought back with him not one ounce of gold. But he brought something far more valuable—a vast hoard of experiences. That one year, spent apparently to so little effect, was to prove another sort of gold-mine, a mine from which Jack London was to extract a rich ore again and again for the rest of his life. His time then had not been wasted. Out in the Klondyke he had used his leisure moments to write, to read, to make notes (for he kept notebooks), to tell stories and to listen to others. More important, he had observed and made *mental* notes of all he had seen. The country of the Klondyke—the Yukon—harsh, cruel and primitive, was to be the setting for so many of his great tales. The rough, tough, rugged types he met there we meet again and again in his later fiction, and not only in those stories set in the far North. The underlying savagery of those parts was to permeate all he wrote. The survival of the fittest, the sheer endurance, whether of man or beast, of those pitted against Nature and against a pitiless society was the theme that ran through book after book. The three Yukon tales included in this collection—*The White Silence, To Build a Fire* and *The Law of Life*—illustrate well this aspect of London's writings. The same theme of struggle—man against severe odds—also runs through such tales as *The Apostate, Make Westing, The Madness of John Harned* and *A Piece of Steak*, all included in this volume.

Jack London now wrote like a man possessed. This time he met with immediate success. Magazine after magazine vied to buy his short stories of the Yukon. At last Jack London the writer had established himself; he was hailed as a new Kipling whose stories were set in the far North instead of British India; he was regarded as the successor of Edgar Allen Poe, the author of *Tales of Mystery and Imagination* and indeed his descriptions of the frozen wastelands can be compared with the scenes of desolation and decay so commonly found in Poe.

Soon his short stories appeared together in book form. *The Son of the Wolf* (1900) won him extraordinary acclaim. One of the earlier tales in this collection, *The White Silence* is taken from it. The important thing for Jack London was that he was now freed from financial worries. Publishers had such great confidence in him that they were now willing to provide him with a regular and comfortable income against the promise of stories to come. At this stage in his life Jack London married; clearly he saw that he could do so with the certainty of avoiding the precarious situation that had been his father's lot: moreover he continued to provide for his mother. Two more successful volumes of tales, *The Children of the Frost* and *The God of his Fathers* were soon followed by his most famous story *The Call of The Wild*, a tale he developed originally from an idea for a short story.

The Call of the Wild (1903) was soon an established classic; it is doubtful whether any work of fiction ever attained such a status so quickly. It told the tale of a domesticated dog that reverts to savagery. Three years later he wrote *White Fang* in which the situation was reversed; this time a savage wolf was won over to domestication. With the publication of these two books and *The Sea-Wolf* (1904) Jack London's reputation was made.

Meanwhile his personal affairs went from bad to worse. He was divorced and remarried. He put his money into property—an odd thing for an avowed Socialist to do (perhaps he wanted to beat the capitalists at their own game). Fame as a writer and wealth from his writings; these were his aims in life. He spent a small fortune on the building of a forty-five foot sailing boat *The Snark*. Everything went wrong with this venture. He was clearly cheated over it, and nearly ruined in the process. However he set off in her to the Pacific in the summer of 1907, leaving behind a trail of debts and his affairs in a precarious state.

From the voyage came two great novels, *Martin Eden*, a very autobiographical story, and *Adventure*, as well as a host of other stories, particularly his *South Sea Tales*. *The Terrible Solomons* and *Make Westing* are fair samples of these; both are included in this collection. His Pacific tales reflected quite uncannily the characters of the peoples around whom they were written: the Melanesians of the Solomons, cruel, barbaric, cunning, sadistic; the Polynesians of Hawaii, gentler, warmer, more tender. It is interesting that from now on Jack London shifted the locale of many of his stories from the Arctic to the South Seas, and for a very good reason: he needed money from writing. To many he was still associated with the Yukon and, as memories of the Klondyke passed from people's minds, there was a real danger that he might easily become forgotten too. Thus it was that, true to form, Jack London rallied. By 1911 he was again in a strong financial position; whereupon he indulged in an orgy of buying and spending. As well as building a luxury ranch on a 1500-acre estate where he entertained lavishly anybody and everybody who cared to visit him—many to cheat and sponge on him—he had embarked on the construction of Wolf House, an almost palace-like home. He was employing a staff of over a hundred with a wages bill of 3000 dollars a month—about £1000, a great deal even for that time. This could not go on. Then to add to his worries in 1913 his great new house, at last completed was burnt down. And London was caught uninsured.

A few more novels followed, notably *John Barleycorn* and *The Mutiny on the Elsinore*, but London's career as a writer was now at an end. For the past three years he had been more businessman than writer, and not very business*like* in the process. He was seized with delusions of grandeur, of wild and impossible schemes and dreams. Heavy drinking, overwork, his constant preoccupation with his recurring financial and domestic crises, plus his now rapidly sinking literary reputation all took their toll. A sick man suffering from now almost unendurable attacks of uraemia he began to find things too much for him. One night, 22nd November 1916, he took an overdose of morphine, whether to deaden his pain or to escape for good from the world and his worries we shall never know. The news of his death made a greater impact on the newspapers of the world than that of the Emperor Franz Joseph of Austria the day before.

One reason for the uneven quality of Jack London's writing has been hinted at: his inability to be selective in what he read, or, to put it another way, to distinguish the worthwhile from the puerile. Another factor was his chequered education—the need to put family before friends, and bread-and-butter before books, as well as several changes of school as the London family slithered down the social scale from prosperous farmstead to waterfront shanty over a period of fourteen years. His habit of writing to a rigid timetable of a thousand words every morning, with little time left for revision—and all his novels, without exception, need revision—left its mark on his work too. This habit he had acquired while at school, where he was excused the morning's singing lesson, for which he had no aptitude at all, but was given a composition to do each day instead. Jack London willed himself to write as he willed himself to read and educate himself, for in his writing he saw the opportunities of both wealth and fame. It was also a form of escapism for him (and he remained an escapist all his life), just as reading and sailing had been forms of escape in his youth from the miseries and poverty of the London household.

Yet despite this unevenness Jack London's writing has many great qualities that more than compensated for its weakness. Chief, of course, is his imagination. This was based partly upon his observation and experience, but he invested it all with a great liveliness and feeling of relentless activity. He had at various periods of his life taken on journalistic assignments (he went, for instance, to report the Russo-Japanese war of 1904), and it is this quality that stands out in his writing—the feeling that he is vividly reporting the events he is describing. He was essentially a man of action, though an idealist in politics, and the titles of many of his books indicate the violent form that much of this action took: *The Abysmal Brute*, *Strength of the Strong*, *White Fang*, *Call of the Wild*, *The Sea-Wolf*. It is an interesting fact that he was known to his intimate friends as 'Wolf' and even signed himself thus when writing to them. Then too the theme of struggle pervades many of his novels: prehistoric savagery in *Before Adam*; a writer's struggles in *Martin Eden*; a man's struggle against liquor in *John Barleycorn* (a book that had a powerful influence in the introduction of the Prohibition laws in the United States); a man's struggle with himself in *The Sea-Wolf*; the struggles of a prizefighter in *The Game*. The list is endless. Restless physical energy runs through all his works, through his short stories just as much as his novels. It was an early ambition of Jack London that one day he would write the story of his own life. It was an ambition that never came to fruition, but the title he planned to give it— *Sailor on Horseback*—is always associated with his name, so varied were his adventures by land and sea.

His influence on such modern American writers as John Steinbeck and Ernest Hemingway was considerable. They too wrote stories and novels that moved, with lots of manly action, and certainly Hemingway himself lived as adventurous and dangerous a life as Jack London. Cannery Row to John Steinbeck was what the Oakland waterfront was to Jack London; and where Jack London sought out adventure in the Yukon or the Pacific, Ernest Hemingway found it in such places as Civil War Spain, Resistance France, Cuba, or Africa.

Even Jack London's sense of humour had a touch of the macabre about it. He could make a joke of cannibalism, or of atrocities. Where Edgar Allen Poe makes us shiver, Jack London makes us chuckle; his humour is cruel and savage. Then, too, because he wrote of life as he saw it, some of his tales of the less fortunate members of society can often evoke a wry smile. See, for instance, *Semper Idem* (the sort of story with a punch-like ending that O. Henry was famed for), or *Told in the Drooling Ward*, in this volume. One thing is certain, the sort of story Jack London wrote was certainly a great contrast to the artificial romantic fiction being turned out in America in his own day, which explains why he received such immediate attention and acclaim.

The experiences of Jack London's early years as a teenager, and later on as a student and one of the unemployed, had taught that life in the 'civilized' world, particularly in the cities, could be just as rough, just as tough, just as savage, just as cruel for the underdog as it was in the frozen Yukon. In both cases there was a struggle for survival, a fight against severe odds with a clear victor, a superman (or superdog) emerging. I have already mentioned the idea of struggle against frustration in a boy's first employment in *The Apostate*. In *A Piece of Steak* he has the same theme, but this time the central figure is a boxer, a prizefighter in poor physical condition against whom the odds are weighted from the start. Here we have man pitted against man, with the one in better physical shape the victor (the 'survival of the fittest' theory in parable form). Bull-fighting was another of his interests (as it was later of Ernest Hemingway); again a fight for survival, this time of man against beast, as in *The Madness of John Harned*. This ability to depict the face of struggle in so many varied ways was perhaps his greatest quality.

I hope that this selection of London's short stories will show what a truly wide range he had; that he was not just the author of *The Call of the Wild*; merely the writer who was associated with the Yukon as Kipling was with India.

In arranging the order of the stories I have been guided by the events of London's own life rather than the order in which he wrote them; though in some cases the two are roughly the same. Thus I have started with one of his 'Fish Patrol' Tales recalling his teenage years, before going with him to the Klondyke in three of his 'Yukon' tales. Next we return home with him and in three further tales look at the lives of the underprivileged in the cities. Then across the Pacific, at the same time looking at other forms of fighting and struggle, prizefighting and bullfighting. Finally a dip into the future in *The Unparalleled Invasion*.

J.T.

White and Yellow

San Francisco Bay is so large that often its storms are more disastrous to ocean-going craft than is the ocean itself in its violent moments. The waters of the bay contain all manner of fish, wherefore its surface is ploughed by the keels of all manner of fishing boats manned by all manner of fishermen. To protect the fish from this motley floating population many wise laws have been passed, and there is a fish patrol to see that these laws are enforced. Exciting times are the lot of the fish patrol: in its history more than one dead patrolman has marked defeat, and more often dead fishermen across their illegal nets have marked success.

Wildest among the fisher-folk may be accounted the Chinese shrimp-catchers. It is the habit of the shrimp to crawl along the bottom in vast armies till it reaches fresh water, when it turns about and crawls back again to the salt. And where the tide ebbs and flows, the Chinese sink great bag-nets to the bottom, with gaping mouths, into which the shrimp crawls and from which it is transferred to the boiling-pot. This in itself would not be bad, were it not for the small mesh of the nets, so small that the tiniest fishes, little new-hatched things not a quarter of an inch long, cannot pass through. The beautiful beaches of Points Pedro and Pablo, where are the shrimp-catchers' villages, are made fearful by the stench from myriads of decaying fish, and against this wasteful destruction it has ever been the duty of the fish patrol to act.

When I was a youngster of sixteen, a good sloop-sailor and all-round bay-waterman, my sloop, the *Reindeer*, was chartered by the Fish Commission, and I became for the time being a deputy patrolman. After a deal of work among the Greek fishermen of the Upper Bay and rivers, where knives flashed at the beginning of trouble and men permitted themselves to be made prisoners only after a revolver was thrust in their faces, we hailed with delight an expedition to the Lower Bay against the Chinese shrimp-catchers.

There were six of us, in two boats, and to avoid suspicion we ran down after dark and dropped anchor under a projecting bluff of land known as Point Pinole. As the east paled with the first light of dawn we got under way again, and hauled close on the land breeze as we slanted across the bay towards Point Pedro. The morning mists curled and clung to the water so that we could see nothing, but we busied ourselves driving the chill from our bodies with hot coffee. Also we had to devote ourselves to the miserable task of bailing, for in some incomprehensible way the *Reindeer* had sprung a generous leak. Half the night had been spent in overhauling the ballast and exploring the seams, but the labour had been without avail. The water still poured in, and perforce we doubled up in the cockpit and tossed it out again.

After coffee, three of the men withdrew to the other boat, a Columbia River salmon boat, leaving three of us in the *Reindeer*. Then the two craft proceeded in company till the sun showed over the eastern sky-line. Its fiery rays dispelled the clinging vapours, and there, before our eyes, like a picture, lay the shrimp fleet, spread out in a great half-moon, the tips of the crescent fully three miles apart, and each junk moored fast to the buoy of a shrimp net. But there was no stir, no sign of life.

The situation dawned upon us. While waiting for slack water, in which to lift their heavy nets from the bed of the bay, the Chinese had all gone to sleep below. We were elated, and our plan of battle was swiftly formed.

'Throw each of your two men on to a junk,' whispered Le Grant to me from the salmon boat. 'And you make fast to a third yourself. We'll do the same, and there's no reason in the world why we shouldn't capture six junks at the least.'

Then we separated. I put the *Reindeer* about on the other tack, ran up under the lee of a junk, shivered the mainsail into the wind and lost headway, and forged past the stern of the junk so slowly and so near that one of the patrolmen stepped lightly aboard. Then I kept off, filled the mainsail, and bore away for a second junk.

Up to this time there had been no noise, but from the first junk captured by the salmon boat an uproar now broke forth. There was shrill Oriental yelling, a pistol shot, and more yelling.

'It's all up. They're warning the others,' said George, the remaining patrolman, as he stood beside me in the cockpit.

By this time we were in the thick of the fleet, and the alarm was spreading with incredible swiftness. The decks were beginning to swarm with half-awakened and half-naked Chinese. Cries and yells of warning and anger were flying over the quiet water, and somewhere a conch shell was being blown with great success. To the right of us I saw the captain of a junk chop away his mooring line with an axe and spring to help his crew at the hoisting of the huge, outlandish lug-sail. But to the left the first heads were popping up from below on another junk, and I rounded up the *Reindeer* alongside long enough for George to spring aboard.

The whole fleet was now under way. In addition to the sails they had gotten out long sweeps, and the bay was being ploughed in every direction by the fleeing junks. I was now alone in the *Reindeer*, seeking feverishly to capture a third prize. The first junk I took after was a clean miss, for it trimmed its sheets and shot away surprisingly into the wind. By fully half a point it outpointed the *Reindeer*, and I began to feel respect for the clumsy craft. Realizing the hopelessness of the pursuit, I filled away, threw out the main-sheet, and drove down before the wind upon the junks to leeward, where I had them at a disadvantage.

The one I had selected wavered indecisively before me, and, as I swung wide to make the boarding gentle, filled suddenly and darted away, the smart Mongols shouting a wild rhythm as they bent to the sweeps. But I had been ready for this. I luffed suddenly. Putting the tiller hard down, and holding it down with my body, I brought the main-sheet in, hand over hand, on the run, so as to retain all possible striking force. The two starboard sweeps of the junk were crumpled up, and then the two boats came together with a crash. The *Reindeer*'s bowsprit, like a monstrous hand, reached over and ripped out the junk's chunky mast and towering sail.

This was met by a curdling yell of rage. A big Chinaman, remarkably evil-looking, with his head swathed in a yellow silk handkerchief and face badly pock-marked, planted a pike-pole on the *Reindeer*'s bow and began to shove the entangled boats apart. Pausing long enough to let go the jib halyards, and just as the *Reindeer* cleared and began to drift astern, I leaped aboard the junk with a line and made fast. He of the yellow handkerchief and pock-marked face came toward me threateningly, but I put my hand into my hip pocket, and he hesitated. I was unarmed, but the Chinese have learned to be fastidiously careful of American hip pockets, and it was upon this that I depended to keep him and his savage crew at a distance.

I ordered him to drop the anchor at the junk's bow, to which he replied, 'No sabbe.' The crew responded in like fashion, and though I made my meaning plain by signs, they refused to understand. Realizing the inexpediency of discussing the matter, I went forward myself, overran the line, and let the anchor go.

'Now get aboard, four of you,' I said in a loud voice, indicating with my fingers that four of them were to go with me and the fifth was to remain by the junk. The Yellow Handkerchief hesitated; but I repeated the order fiercely (much more fiercely than I felt), at the same time sending my hand to my hip. Again the Yellow Handkerchief was overawed, and with surly looks he led three of his men aboard the *Reindeer*. I cast off at once, and, leaving the jib down, steered a course for George's junk. Here it was easier, for there were two of us, and George had a pistol to fall back on if it came to the worst. And here, as with my junk, four Chinese were transferred to the sloop and one left behind to take care of things.

Four more were added to our passenger list from the third junk. By this time the salmon boat had collected its twelve prisoners and came alongside, badly overloaded. To make matters worse, as it was a small boat, the patrolmen were so jammed in with their prisoners that they would have little chance in case of trouble.

'You'll have to help us out,' said Le Grant.

I looked over my prisoners, who had crowded into the cabin and on top of it. 'I can take three,' I answered.

'Make it four,' he suggested, 'and I'll take Bill with me.' (Bill was the third patrolman.) 'We haven't elbow room here, and in case of a scuffle one white to every two of them will be just about the right proportion.'

The exchange was made, and the salmon boat got up its spritsail and headed down the bay towards the marshes off San Rafael. I ran up the jib and followed with the *Reindeer*. San Rafael, where we were to turn our catch over to the authorities, communicated with the bay by way of a long and tortuous slough, or marshland creek, which could be navigated only when the tide was in. Slack water had come, and, as the ebb was commencing, there was need for hurry if we cared to escape waiting half a day for the next tide.

But the land breeze had begun to die away with the rising sun, and now came only in failing puffs. The salmon boat got out its oars and soon left us far astern. Some of the Chinese stood in the forward part of the cockpit, near the cabin doors, and once, as I leaned over the cockpit rail to flatten down the jib-sheet a bit, I felt some one brush against my hip pocket. I made no sign, but out of the corner of my eye I saw that the Yellow Handkerchief had discovered the emptiness of the pocket which had hitherto overawed him.

To make matters serious, during all the excitement of boarding the junks the *Reindeer* had not been bailed, and the water was beginning to slush over the cockpit floor. The shrimp-catchers pointed at it and looked to me questioningly.

'Yes,' I said. 'Bime by, allee same dlown, velly quick, you no bail now. Sabbe?'

No, they did not 'sabbe', or at least they shook their heads to that effect, though they chattered most comprehendingly to one another in their own lingo. I pulled up three or four of the bottom boards, got a couple of buckets from a locker, and by unmistakable sign-language invited them to fall to. But they laughed, and some crowded into the cabin and some climbed up on top.

Their laughter was not good laughter. There was a hint of menace in it, a maliciousness which their black looks verified. The Yellow Handkerchief, since his discovery of my empty pocket, had become most insolent in his bearing, and he wormed about among the other prisoners, talking to them with great earnestness.

Swallowing my chagrin, I stepped down into the cockpit and began throwing out the water. But hardly had I begun, when the boom swung overhead, the mainsail filled with a jerk, and the *Reindeer* heeled over. The day wind was springing up. George was the veriest of landlubbers, so I was forced to give over bailing and take the tiller. The wind was blowing directly off Point Pedro and the high mountains behind, and because of this was squally and uncertain, half the time belly-ing the canvas out and the other half flapping it idly.

George was about the most all-round helpless man I had ever met. Among his other disabilities, he was a consumptive, and I knew that if he attempted to bail, it might bring on a haemorrhage. Yet the rising water warned me that something must be done. Again I ordered the shrimp-catchers to lend a hand with the buckets. They laughed defiantly, and those inside the cabin, the water up to their ankles, shouted back and forth with those on top.

'You'd better get out your gun and make them bail,' I said to George.

But he shook his head and showed all too plainly that he was afraid. The Chinese could see the funk he was in as well as I could, and their insolence became insufferable. Those in the cabin broke into the food lockers, and those above scrambled down and joined them in a feast on our crackers and canned goods.

'What do we care?' George said weakly.

I was fuming with helpless anger. 'If they get out of hand, it will be too late to care. The best thing you can do is to get them in check right now.'

The water was rising higher and higher, and the gusts, fore-runners of a steady breeze, were growing stiffer and stiffer. And between the gusts, the prisoners, having gotten away with a week's grub, took to crowding first to one side and then to the other till the *Reindeer* rocked like a cockle-shell. Yellow Hand-kerchief approached me, and, pointing out his village on the Point Pedro beach, gave me to understand that if I turned the *Reindeer* in that direction and put them ashore, they, in turn, would go to bailing. By now the water in the cabin was up to the bunks, and the bed-clothes were sopping. It was a foot deep on the cockpit floor. Nevertheless I refused, and I could see by George's face that he was disappointed.

'If you don't show some nerve, they'll rush us and throw us overboard,' I said to him. 'Better give me your revolver, if you want to be safe.'

'The safest thing to do,' he chattered cravenly, 'is to put them ashore. I, for one, don't want to be drowned for the sake of a handful of dirty Chinamen.'

'And I, for another, don't care to give in to a handful of dirty Chinamen to escape drowning,' I answered hotly.

'You'll sink the *Reindeer* under us all at this rate,' he whined. 'And what good that'll do I can't see.'

'Every man to his taste,' I retorted.

He made no reply, but I could see he was trembling pitifully. Between the threatening Chinese and the rising water he was beside himself with fright; and, more than the Chinese and the water, I feared him and what his fright might impel him to do. I could see him casting longing glances at the small skiff towing astern, so in the next calm I hauled the skiff alongside. As I did so his eyes brightened with hope; but before he could guess my intention, I stove the frail bottom through with a hand-axe, and the skiff filled to its gunwales.

'It's sink or float together,' I said. 'And if you'll give me your revolver, I'll have the *Reindeer* bailed out in a jiffy.'

'They're too many for us,' he whimpered. 'We can't fight them all.'

I turned my back on him in disgust. The salmon boat had long since passed from sight behind a little archipelago known as the Marin Islands, so no help could be looked for from that quarter. Yellow Handkerchief came up to me in a familiar manner, the water in the cockpit slushing against his legs. I did not like his looks. I felt that beneath the pleasant smile he was trying to put on his face there was an ill purpose. I ordered him back, and so sharply that he obeyed.

'Now keep your distance,' I commanded, 'and don't you come closer!'

'Wha' fo'?' he demanded indignantly. 'I t'ink-um talkee talkee heap good.'

'Talkee talkee,' I answered bitterly, for I knew now that he had understood all that passed between George and me. 'What for talkee talkee? You no sabbe talkee talkee.'

He grinned in a sickly fashion.'Yep, I sabbe velly much. I honest Chinaman.'

'All right,' I answered. 'You sabbe talkee talkee, then you bail water plenty plenty. After that we talkee talkee.'

He shook his head, at the same time pointing over his shoulder to his comrades. 'No can do. Velly bad Chinamen, heap velly bad. I t'ink-um—'

'Stand back!' I shouted, for I had noticed his hand disappear beneath his blouse and his body prepare for a spring.

Disconcerted, he went back into the cabin, to hold a council, apparently, from the way the jabbering broke forth. The *Reindeer* was very deep in the water, and her movements had grown quite loggy. In a rough sea she would have inevitably swamped; but the wind, when it did blow, was off the land, and scarcely a ripple disturbed the surface of the bay.

'I think you'd better head for the beach,' George said abruptly, in a manner that told me his fear had forced him to make up his mind to some course of action.

'I think not,' I answered shortly.

'I command you,' he said in a bullying tone.

'I was commanded to bring these prisoners into San Rafael,' was my reply.

Our voices were raised, and the sound of the altercation brought the Chinese out of the cabin.

'Now will you head for the beach?'

This from George, and I found myself looking into the muzzle of his revolver—of the revolver he dared to use on me, but was too cowardly to use on the prisoners.

My brain seemed smitten with a dazzling brightness. The whole situation, in all its bearings, was focussed sharply before me—the shame of losing the prisoners, the worthlessness and cowardice of George, the meeting with Le Grant and the other patrol men and the lame explanation; and then there was the fight I had fought so hard, victory wrenched from me just as I thought I had it within my grasp. And out of the tail of my eye I could see the Chinese crowding together by the cabin doors and leering triumphantly. It would never do.

I threw my hand up and my head down. The first act elevated the muzzle, and the second removed my head from the path of the bullet which went whistling past. One hand closed on George's wrist, the other on the revolver. Yellow Handkerchief and his gang sprang toward me. It was now or never. Putting all my strength into a sudden effort, I swung George's body forward to meet them. Then I pulled back with equal suddenness, ripping the revolver out of his fingers and jerking him off his feet. He fell against Yellow Handkerchief's knees, who stumbled over him, and the pair wallowed in the bailing hole where the cockpit floor was torn open. The next instant I was covering them with my revolver, and the wild shrimp-catchers were cowering and cringing away.

But I swiftly discovered that there was all the difference in the world between shooting men who are attacking and men who are doing nothing more than simply refusing to obey. For obey they would not when I ordered them into the bailing hole. I threatened them with the revolver, but they sat stolidly in the flooded cabin and on the roof and would not move.

Fifteen minutes passed, the *Reindeer* sinking deeper and deeper, her mainsail flapping in the calm. But from off the Point Pedro shore I saw a dark line form on the water and travel toward us. It was the steady breeze I had been expecting so long. I called to the Chinese and pointed it out. They hailed it with exclamations. Then I pointed to the sail and to the water in the *Reindeer*, and indicated by signs that when the

wind reached the sail, what of the water aboard we would cap-
size. But they jeered defiantly, for they knew it was in my
power to luff the helm and let go the main-sheet, so as to spill
the wind and escape damage.

But my mind was made up. I hauled in the main-sheet a foot
or two, took a turn with it, and bracing my feet, put my back
against the tiller. This left me one hand for the sheet and one
for the revolver. The dark line drew nearer, and I could see
them looking from me to it and back again with an apprehension
they could not successfully conceal. My brain and will and
endurance were pitted against theirs, and the problem was
which could stand the strain of imminent death the longer and
not give in.

Then the wind struck us. The main-sheet tautened with a
brisk rattling of the blocks, the boom uplifted, the sail bellied
out, and the *Reindeer* heeled over—over, and over, till the
lee-rail went under, the cabin windows went under, and the
bay began to pour in over the cockpit rail. So violently had she
heeled over, that the men in the cabin had been thrown on top
of one another into the lee bunk, where they squirmed and
twisted and were washed about, those underneath being
perilously near to drowning.

The wind freshened a bit, and the *Reindeer* went over
farther than ever. For the moment I thought she was gone, and
I knew that another puff like that and she surely would go.
While I pressed her under and debated whether I should give
up or not, the Chinese cried for mercy. I think it was the sweet-
est sound I have ever heard. And then, and not until then, did
I luff up and ease out the main-sheet. The *Reindeer* righted
very slowly, and when she was on an even keel was so much
awash that I doubted if she could be saved.

But the Chinese scrambled madly into the cockpit and fell to
bailing with buckets, pots, pans, and everything they could lay
hands on. It was a beautiful sight to see that water flying over
the side! And when the *Reindeer* was high and proud on the
water once more, we dashed away with the breeze on our
quarter, and at the last possible moment crossed the mud flats
and entered the slough.

The spirit of the Chinese was broken, and so docile did they
become that ere we made San Rafael they were out with the
tow-rope, Yellow Handkerchief at the head of the line. As for
George, it was his last trip with the fish patrol. He did not care
for that sort of thing, he explained, and he thought a clerkship
ashore was good enough for him. And we thought so too.

The White Silence

'Carmen won't last more than a couple of days.' Mason spat out a chunk of ice and surveyed the poor animal ruefully, then put her foot in his mouth and proceeded to bite out the ice which clustered cruelly between the toes.

The woman threw off her gloom at this, and in her eyes welled up a great love for her white lord—the first white man she had ever seen—the first man whom she had known to treat a woman as something better than a mere animal or beast of burden.

'Yes, Ruth,' continued her husband, having recourse to the macaronic jargon in which it was alone possible for them to understand each other; 'wait till we clean up and pull for the Outside. We'll take the White Man's canoe and go to the Salt Water. Yes, bad water, rough water—great mountains dance up and down all the time. And so big, so far, so far away—you travel ten sleep, twenty sleep, forty sleep'—he graphically enumerated the days on his fingers—'all the time water, bad water. Then you come to great village, plenty people, just the same mosquitoes next summer. Wigwams oh, so high—ten, twenty pines. Hi-yu skookum!'

He paused impotently, cast an appealing glance at Malemute Kid, then laboriously placed the twenty pines, end on end, by sign language. Malemute Kid smiled with cheery cynicism; but Ruth's eyes were wide with wonder, and with pleasure; for she half believed he was joking, and such condescension pleased her poor woman's heart.

'And then you step into a—a box, and pouf! up you go.' He tossed his empty cup in the air by way of illustration and, as he deftly caught it, cried: 'And biff! down you come. Oh, great medicine men! You go Fort Yukon, I go Arctic City—twenty-five sleep—big string, all the time—I catch him—string I say, 'Hello, Ruth! How are ye?'—and you say, 'Is that my good husband?'—and I say, 'Yes'—and you say, 'No can bake good bread, no more soda'—then I say, 'Look in cache, under flour; good-bye.' You look and catch plenty soda. All the time you Fort Yukon, me Arctic City. Hi-yu medicine man!'

Ruth smiled so ingenuously at the fairy story that both men burst into laughter. A row among the dogs cut short the wonders of the Outside, and by the time the snarling combatants were separated, she had lashed the sleds and all was ready for the trail.

'Mush! Baldy! Hi! Mush on!' Mason worked his whip smartly and, as the dogs whined low in the traces, broke out the sled with the gee pole. Ruth followed with the second team, leaving Malemute Kid, who had helped her start, to bring up the rear. Strong man, brute that he was, capable of felling an ox at a blow, he could not bear to beat the poor animals, but humoured them as a dog driver rarely does—nay, almost wept with them in their misery.

'Come, mush on there, you poor sore-footed brutes!' he murmured, after several ineffectual attempts to start the load. But his patience was at last rewarded, and though whimpering with pain, they hastened to join their fellows.

No more conversation; the toil of the trail will not permit such extravagance. And of all deadening labours, that of the Northland trail is the worst. Happy is the man who can weather a day's travel at the price of silence, and that on a beaten track.

And of all heartbreaking labours, that of breaking trail is the worst. At every step the great webbed shoe sinks till the snow is level with the knee. Then up, straight up, the deviation of a fraction of an inch being a certain precursor of disaster, the snowshoe must be lifted till the surface is cleared; then forward, down, and the other foot is raised perpendicularly for the matter of half a yard. He who tries this for the first time, if haply he avoids bringing his shoes in dangerous propinquity and measures not his length on the treacherous footing, will give up exhausted at the end of a hundred yards; he who can

keep out of the way of the dogs for a whole day may well crawl
into his sleeping bag with a clear conscience and a pride which
passeth all understanding; and he who travels twenty sleeps on
the Long Trail is a man whom the gods may envy.

The afternoon wore on, and with the awe, born of the White
Silence, the voiceless travellers bent to their work. Nature has
many tricks wherewith she convinces man of his finity—the
ceaseless flow of the tides, the fury of the storm, the shock of
the earthquake, the long roll of heaven's artillery—but the
most tremendous, the most stupefying of all, is the passive
phase of the White Silence. All movement ceases, the sky clears,
the heavens are as brass; the slightest whisper seems sacrilege,
and man becomes timid, affrighted at the sound of his own
voice. Sole speck of life journeying across the ghostly wastes of
a dead world, he trembles at his audacity, realizes that his is a
maggot's life, nothing more. Strange thoughts arise unsum-
moned, and the mystery of all things strives for utterance. And
the fear of death, of God, of the universe, comes over him—
the hope of the Resurrection and the Life, the yearning for
immortality, the vain striving of the imprisoned essence—it is
then, if ever, man walks alone with God.

So wore the day away. The river took a great bend, and
Mason headed his team for the cutoff across the narrow neck of
land. But the dogs balked at the high bank. Again and again,
though Ruth and Malemute Kid were shoving on the sled, they
slipped back. Then came the concerted effort. The miserable
creatures, weak from hunger, exerted their last strength. Up—
up—the sled poised on the top of the bank; but the leader
swung the string of dogs behind him to the right, fouling
Mason's shoes. The result was grievous. Mason was whipped
off his feet; one of the dogs fell in the traces; and the sled
toppled back, dragging everything to the bottom again.

Slash! the whip fell among the dogs savagely, especially upon
the one which had fallen.

'Don't Mason,' entreated Malemute Kid; 'the poor devil's
on its last legs. Wait and we'll put my team on.'

Mason deliberately withheld the whip till the last word had
fallen, then out flashed the long lash, completely curling about
the offending creature's body. Carmen—for it was Carmen—
cowered in the snow, cried piteously, then rolled over on her
side.

It was a tragic moment, a pitiful incident of the trail—a
dying dog, two comrades in anger. Ruth glanced solicitously
from man to man. But Malemute Kid restrained himself,

though there was a world of reproach in his eyes, and, bending over the dog, cut the traces. No word was spoken. The teams were double-spanned and the difficulty overcome; the sleds were under way again, the dying dog dragging herself along in the rear. As long as an animal can travel, it is not shot, and this last chance is accorded it—the crawling into camp, if it can, in the hope of a moose being killed.

Already penitent for his angry action, but too stubborn to make amends, Mason toiled on at the head of the cavalcade, little dreaming that danger hovered in the air. The timber clustered thick in the sheltered bottom, and through this they threaded their way. Fifty feet or more from the trail towered a lofty pine. For generations it had stood there, and for generations destiny had this one end in view—perhaps the same had been decreed of Mason.

He stooped to fasten the loosened thong of his moccasin. The sleds came to a halt, and the dogs lay down in the snow without a whimper. The stillness was weird; not a breath rustled the frost-encrusted forest; the cold and silence of outer space had chilled the heart and smote the trembling lips of nature. A sigh pulsed through the air—they did not seem to actually hear it, but rather felt it, like the premonition of movement in a motionless void. Then the great tree, burdened with its weight of years and snow, played its last part in the tragedy of life. He heard the warning crash and attempted to spring up but, almost erect, caught the blow squarely on the shoulder.

The sudden danger, the quick death—how often had Malemute Kid faced it! The pine needles were still quivering as he gave his commands and sprang into action. Nor did the Indian girl faint or raise her voice in idle wailing, as might many of her white sisters. At his order, she threw her weight on the end of a quickly extemporized handspike, easing the pressure and listening to her husband's groans, while Malemute Kid attacked the tree with his axe. The steel rang merrily as it bit into the frozen trunk, each stroke being accompanied by a forced, audible respiration, the 'Huh!' 'Huh!' of the woodsman.

At last the Kid laid the pitiable thing that was once a man in the snow. But worse than his comrade's pain was the dumb anguish in the woman's face, the blended look of hopeful, hopeless query. Little was said; those of the Northland are early taught the futility of words and the inestimable value of deeds. With the temperature at sixty-five below zero, a man cannot lie many minutes in the snow and live. So the sled lashings were cut, and the sufferer, rolled in furs, laid on a couch of boughs. Before him roared a fire, built of the very wood which wrought the mishap. Behind and partially over him was stretched the primitive fly—a piece of canvas, which caught the radiating heat and threw it back and down at him— a trick which men may know who study physics at the fount.

And men who have shared their bed with death know when the call is sounded. Mason was terribly crushed. The most cursory examination revealed it. His right arm, leg, and back were broken; his limbs were paralysed from the hips; and the likelihood of internal injuries was large. An occasional moan was his only sign of life.

No hope; nothing to be done. The pitiless night crept slowly by—Ruth's portion, the despairing stoicism of her race, and Malemute Kid adding new lines to his face of bronze. In fact, Mason suffered least of all, for he spent his time in eastern Tennessee, in the Great Smoky Mountains, living over the scenes of his childhood. And most pathetic was the melody of his long-forgotten Southern vernacular, as he raved of swimming holes and coon hunts and water-melon raids. It was as Greek to Ruth, but the Kid understood and felt—felt as only one can feel who has been shut out for years from all that civilization means.

Morning brought consciousness to the stricken man, and Malemute Kid bent closer to catch his whispers.

'You remember when we forgathered on the Tanana, four years come next ice run? I didn't care so much for her then. It was more like she was pretty, and there was a smack of excitement about it, I think. But d'ye know, I've come to think a heap of her. She's been a good wife to me, always at my shoulder in the pinch. And when it comes to trading, you know there isn't her equal! D'ye recollect the time she shot the Moosehorn Rapids to pull you and me off that rock, the bullets whipping the water like hailstones?—and the time of the famine at Nuklukyeto?—or when she raced the ice run to bring the news? Yes, she's been a good wife to me, better'n that other one. Didn't know I'd been there? Never told you, eh? Well, I tried it once, down in the States. That's why I'm here. Been raised together, too. I came away to give her a chance for divorce. She got it.

'But that's got nothing to do with Ruth. I had thought of cleaning up and pulling for the Outside next year—her and I— but it's too late. Don't send her back to her people, Kid. It's beastly hard for a woman to go back. Think of it!—nearly four years on our bacon and beans and flour and dried fruit, and then to go back to her fish and caribou. It's not good for her to have tried our ways, to come to know they're better'n her people's, and then return to them. Take care of her, Kid— why don't you—but no, you always fought shy of them—and you never told me why you came to this country. Be kind to her and send her back to the States as soon as you can. But fix it so she can come back—liable to get homesick, you know.

'And the youngster—it's drawn us closer, Kid. I only hope it is a boy. Think of it!—flesh of my flesh, Kid. He mustn't stop in this country. And if it's a girl, why, she can't. Sell my furs; they'll fetch at least five thousand, and I've got as much more with the company. And handle my interests with yours. I think that bench claim will show up. See that he gets a good schooling; and, Kid, above all, don't let him come back. This country was not made for white men.

'I'm a gone man, Kid. Three or four sleeps at the best. You've got to go on. You must go on! Remember, it's my wife, it's my boy—O God! I hope it's a boy! You can't stay by me— and I charge you, a dying man, to pull on.'

'Give me three days,' pleaded Malemute Kid. 'You may change for the better; something may turn up.

'No.'

'Just three days.'

'You must pull on.'

'Two days.'

'It's my wife and my boy, Kid. You would not ask it.'

'One day.'

'No, no! I charge—'

'Only one day. We can shave it through on the grub, and I might knock over a moose.'

'No—all right; one day, but not a minute more. And, Kid, don't—don't leave me to face it alone. Just a shot, one pull on the trigger. You understand. Think of it! Think of it! Flesh of my flesh, and I'll never live to see him!

'Send Ruth here. I want to say good-bye and tell her that she must think of the boy and not wait till I'm dead. She might refuse to go with you if I didn't. Good-bye, old man; good-bye.

'Kid! I say—a—sink a hole above the pup, next to the slide. I panned out forty cents on my shovel there.

'And, Kid!' He stooped lower to catch the last faint words, the dying man's surrender of his pride. 'I'm sorry—for—you know—Carmen.'

Leaving the girl crying softly over her man, Malemute Kid slipped into his parka and snowshoes, tucked his rifle under his arm, and crept away into the forest. He was no tyro in the stern sorrows of the Northland, but never had he faced so stiff a problem as this. In the abstract, it was a plain, mathematical proposition—three possible lives as against one doomed one. But now he hesitated. For five years, shoulder to shoulder, on the rivers and trails, in the camps and mines, facing death by field and flood and famine, had they knitted the bonds of their comradeship. So close was the tie that he had often been conscious of a vague jealousy of Ruth, from the first time she had come between. And now it must be severed by his own hand.

Though he prayed for a moose, just one moose, all game seemed to have deserted the land, and nightfall found the exhausted man crawling into camp, light-handed, heavy-hearted. An uproar from the dogs and shrill cries from Ruth hastened him.

Bursting into the camp, he saw the girl in the midst of the snarling pack, laying about her with an axe. The dogs had broken the iron rule of their masters and were rushing the grub. He joined the issue with his rifle reversed, and the hoary game of natural selection was played out with all the ruthlessness of its primeval environment. Rifle and axe went up and down, hit or missed with monotonous regularity; lithe bodies flashed, with wild eyes and dripping fangs; and man and beast fought for supremacy to the bitterest conclusion. Then the beaten brutes crept to the edge of the firelight, licking their wounds, voicing their misery to the stars.

The whole stock of dried salmon had been devoured, and perhaps five pounds of flour remained to tide them over two hundred miles of wilderness. Ruth returned to her husband, while Malemute Kid cut up the warm body of one of the dogs, the skull of which had been crushed by the axe. Every portion was carefully put away, save the hide and offal, which were cast to his fellows of the moment before.

Morning brought fresh trouble. The animals were turning on each other. Carmen, who still clung to her slender thread of life, was downed by the pack. The lash fell among them unheeded. They cringed and cried under the blows, but refused to scatter till the last wretched bit had disappeared—bones, hide, hair, everything.

Malemute Kid went about his work, listening to Mason,

who was back in Tennessee, delivering tangled discourses and wild exhortations to his brethren of other days.

Taking advantage of neighbouring pines, he worked rapidly, and Ruth watched him make a cache similar to those sometimes used by hunters to preserve their meat from the wolverines and dogs. One after the other, he bent the tops of two small pines towards each other and nearly to the ground, making them fast with thongs of moosehide. Then he beat the dogs into submission, and harnessed them to two of the sleds, loading the same with everything but the furs which enveloped Mason. These he wrapped and lashed tightly about him, fastening either end of the ropes to the bent pines. A single stroke of his hunting knife would release them and send the body high in the air.

Ruth had received her husband's last wishes and made no struggle. Poor girl, she had learned the lesson of obedience well. From a child, she had bowed, and seen all women bow, to the lords of creation, and it did not seem in the nature of things for woman to resist. The Kid permitted her one outburst of grief, as she kissed her husband—her own people had no such custom—then led her to the foremost sled and helped her into her snowshoes. Blindly, instinctively, she took the gee pole and whip, and 'mushed' the dogs out on the trail. Then he returned to Mason, who had fallen into a coma, and long after she was out of sight crouched by the fire, waiting, hoping, praying for his comrade to die.

It is not pleasant to be alone with painful thoughts in the White Silence. The silence of gloom is merciful, shrouding one as with protection and breathing a thousand tangible sympathies; but the bright White Silence, clear and cold, under steely skies, is pitiless.

An hour passed—two hours—but the man would not die. At high noon the sun, without raising its rim above the southern horizon, threw a suggestion of fire athwart the heavens, then quickly drew it back. Malemute Kid roused and dragged himself to his comrade's side. He cast one glance about him. The White Silence seemed to sneer, and a great fear came upon him. There was a sharp report; Mason swung into his aerial sepulchre, and Malemute Kid lashed the dogs into a wild gallop as he fled across the snow.

To Build a Fire

Day had broken cold and grey, exceedingly cold and grey, when the man turned aside from the main Yukon trail and climbed the high earth-bank, where a dim and little-travelled trail led eastward through the fat spruce timberland. It was a steep bank, and he paused for breath at the top, excusing the act to himself by looking at his watch. It was nine o'clock. There was no sun nor hint of sun, though there was not a cloud in the sky. It was a clear day, and yet there seemed an intangible pall over the face of things, a subtle gloom that made the day dark, and that was due to the absence of sun. This fact did not worry the man. He was used to the lack of sun. It had been days since he had seen the sun, and he knew that a few more days must pass before that cheerful orb, due south, would just peep above the skyline and dip immediately from view.

The man flung a look back along the way he had come. The Yukon lay a mile wide and hidden under three feet of ice. On top of this ice were as many feet of snow. It was all pure white, rolling in gentle undulations where the ice jams of the freeze-up had formed. North and south, as far as his eye could see, it was unbroken white, save for a dark hairline that curved and twisted from around the spruce-covered island to the south and that curved and twisted away into the north, where it disappeared behind another spruce-covered island. This dark hairline was the trail—the main trail—that led south five hundred miles to the Chilcoot Pass, Dyea, and salt water; and that led north seventy miles to Dawson, and still on to the north a thousand miles to Nulato, and finally to St. Michael, on Bering Sea, a thousand miles and half a thousand more.

But all this—the mysterious, far-reaching hairline trail, the absence of sun from the sky, the tremendous cold, and the strangeness and weirdness of it all—made no impression on the man. It was not because he was long used to it. He was a new-comer in the land, a *chechaquo*, and this was his first winter. The trouble with him was that he was without imagination. He was quick and alert in the things of life, but only in the things, and not in the significances. Fifty degrees below zero meant eighty-odd degrees of frost. Such fact impressed him as being cold and uncomfortable, and that was all. It did not lead him to meditate upon his frailty as a creature of temperature, and upon man's frailty in general, able only to live within certain narrow limits of heat and cold; and from there on it did not lead him to the conjectural field of immortality and man's place in the universe. Fifty degrees below zero stood for a bite of frost that hurt and that must be guarded against by the use of mittens, ear flaps, warm moccasins, and thick socks. Fifty degrees below zero. That there should be anything more to it than that was a thought that never entered his head.

As he turned to go on, he spat speculatively. There was a sharp explosive crackle that startled him. He spat again. And again, in the air, before it could fall to the snow, the spittle crackled. He knew that at fifty below spittle crackled on the snow, but this spittle had crackled in the air. Undoubtedly it was colder than fifty below—how much colder he did not know. But the temperature did not matter. He was bound for the old claim on the left fork of Henderson Creek, where the boys were already. They had come over across the divide from the Indian Creek country, while he had come the roundabout way to take a look at the possibilities of getting out logs in the spring from the islands in the Yukon. He would be in to camp by six o'clock; a bit after dark, it was true, but the boys would be there, a fire would be going, and a hot supper would be ready. As for lunch, he pressed his hand against the protrud-ing bundle under his jacket. It was also under his shirt, wrap-ped up in a handkerchief and lying against the naked skin. It was the only way to keep the biscuits from freezing. He smiled agreeably to himself as he thought of those biscuits, each cut open and sopped in bacon grease, and each enclosing a generous slice of fried bacon.

He plunged in among the big spruce trees. The trail was faint. A foot of snow had fallen since the last sled had passed over, and he was glad he was without a sled, travelling light. In fact, he carried nothing but the lunch wrapped in the handkerchief. He was surprised, however, at the cold. It certainly was cold, he concluded, as he rubbed his numb nose and cheekbones with his mittened hand. He was a warm-whiskered man, but the hair on his face did not protect the high cheekbones and the eager nose that thrust itself aggressively into the frosty air.

At the man's heels trotted a dog, a big native husky, the proper wolf-dog, grey-coated and without any visible or temperamental difference from its brother, the wild wolf. The animal was depressed by the tremendous cold. It knew that it was no time for travelling. Its instinct told it a truer tale than was told to the man by the man's judgment. In reality, it was not merely colder than fifty below zero; it was colder than sixty below, than seventy below. It was seventy-five below zero. Since the freezing point is thirty-two above zero, it meant that one hundred and seven degrees of frost obtained. The dog did not know anything about thermometers. Possibly in its brain there was no sharp consciousness of a condition of very cold such as was in the man's brain. But the brute had its instinct. It experienced a vague but menacing apprehension that subdued it and made it slink along at the man's heels, and that made it question eagerly every unwonted movement of the man as if expecting him to go into camp or to seek shelter somewhere and build a fire. The dog had learned fire, and it wanted fire, or else to burrow under the snow and cuddle its warmth away from the air.

The frozen moisture of its breathing had settled on its fur in a fine powder of frost, and especially were its jowls, muzzle, and eyelashes whitened by its crystal breath. The man's red beard and moustache were likewise frosted, but more solidly, the deposit taking the form of ice and increasing with every warm, moist breath he exhaled. Also, the man was chewing tobacco, and the muzzle of ice held his lips so rigidly that he was unable to clear his chin when he expelled the juice. The result was a crystal beard of the colour and solidity of amber was increasing its length on his chin. If he fell down it would shatter itself, like glass, into brittle fragments. But he did not mind the appendage. It was the penalty all tobacco chewers paid in that country, and he had been out before in two cold snaps. They had not been so cold as this, he knew, but by the spirit thermometer at Sixty Mile he knew they had been registered at fifty below and at fifty-five.

He held on through the level stretch of woods for several miles, crossed a wide flat of nigger heads, and dropped down a bank to the frozen bed of a small stream. This was Henderson Creek, and he knew he was ten miles from the forks. He looked at his watch. It was ten o'clock. He was making four miles an hour, and he calculated that he would arrive at the forks at half-past twelve. He decided to celebrate that event by eating his lunch there.

The dog dropped in again at his heels, with a tail drooping discouragement, as the man swung along the creek bed. The furrow of the old sled trail was plainly visible, but a dozen inches of snow covered up the marks of the last runners. In a month no man had come up or down that silent creek. The man held steadily on. He was not much given to thinking, and just then particularly he had nothing to think about save that he would eat lunch at the forks and that at six o'clock he would be in camp with the boys. There was nobody to talk to; and, had there been, speech would have been impossible because of the ice muzzle on his mouth. So he continued monotonously to chew tobacco and to increase the length of his amber beard.

Once in a while the thought reiterated itself that it was very cold and that he had never experienced such cold. As he walked along he rubbed his cheekbones and nose with the back of his mittened hand. He did this automatically, now and again changing hands. But, rub as he would, the instant he stopped his cheekbones went numb, and the following instant the end of his nose went numb. He was sure to frost his cheeks; he knew that, and experienced a pang of regret that he had not devised a nose strap of the sort Bud wore in cold snaps. Such a strap passed across the cheeks, as well, and saved them. But it didn't matter much, after all. What were frosted cheeks? A bit painful, that was all; they were never serious.

Empty as the man's mind was of thoughts, he was keenly observant, and he noticed the changes in the creeks, the curves and bends and timber jams, and always he sharply noted where he placed his feet. Once, coming round a bend, he shied abruptly, like a startled horse, curved away from the place where he had been walking, and retreated several paces back along the trail. The creek he knew was frozen clear to the bottom—no creek could contain water in that Arctic winter— but he knew also that there were springs that bubbled out from the hillsides and ran along under the snow and on top of the ice of the creek. He knew that the coldest snaps never froze these springs, and he knew likewise their danger. They were traps. They hid pools of water under the snow that might be three inches deep, or three feet. Sometimes a skin of ice half an inch thick covered them, and in turn was covered by the snow. Sometimes there were alternate layers of water and ice skin, so that when one broke through he kept on breaking through for a while, sometimes wetting himself to the waist.

That was why he had shied in such a panic. He had felt the give under his feet and heard the crackle of a snow-hidden ice skin. And to get his feet wet in such a temperature meant trouble and danger. At the very least it meant delay, for he would be forced to stop and build a fire, and under its protection to bare his feet while he dried his socks and moccasins. He stood and studied the creek bed and its banks, and decided that the flow of water came from the right. He reflected awhile, rubbing his nose and cheeks, then skirted to the left, stepping gingerly and testing the footing for each step. Once clear of the danger, he took a fresh chew of tobacco and swung along at his four-mile gait.

In the course of the next two hours he came upon several similar traps. Usually the snow above the hidden pools had a sunken, candied appearance that advertised the danger. Once again, however, he had a close call; and once, suspecting danger, he compelled the dog to go on in front. The dog did not want to go. It hung back until the man shoved it forward, and then it went quickly across the white, unbroken surface. Suddenly it broke through, floundered to one side, and got away to firmer footing. It had wet its forefeet and legs, and almost immediately the water that clung to it turned to ice. It made quick efforts to lick the ice off its legs, then dropped down in the snow and began to bite out the ice that had formed between the toes. This was a matter of instinct. To permit the ice to remain would mean sore feet. It did not know this. It merely obeyed the mysterious prompting that arose from the deep crypts of its being. But the man knew, having achieved a judgment on the subject, and he removed the mitten from his right hand and helped to tear out the ice particles. He did not expose his fingers more than a minute, and was astonished at the swift numbness that smote them. It certainly was cold. He pulled on the mitten hastily, and beat the hand savagely across his chest.

At twelve o'clock the day was at its brightest. Yet the sun was too far south on its winter journey to clear the horizon.

The bulge of the earth intervened between it and Henderson Creek, where the man walked under a clear sky at noon and cast no shadow. At half-past twelve, to the minute, he arrived at the forks of the creek. He was pleased at the speed he had made. If he kept it up, he would certainly be with the boys by six. He unbuttoned his jacket and shirt and drew forth his lunch. The action consumed no more than a quarter of a minute, yet in that brief moment the numbness laid hold of the exposed fingers. He did not put the mitten on, but, instead, struck the fingers a dozen sharp smashes against his leg. Then he sat down on a snow-covered log to eat. The sting that followed upon the striking of his fingers against his leg ceased so quickly that he was startled. He had had no chance to take a bite of biscuit. He struck the fingers repeatedly and returned them to the mitten, baring the other hand for the purpose of eating. He tried to take a mouthful, but the ice muzzle prevented. He had forgotten to build a fire and thaw out. He chuckled at his foolishness, and as he chuckled he noted the numbness creeping into the exposed fingers. Also, he noted that the stinging which had first come to his toes when he sat down was already passing away. He wondered whether the toes were warm or numb. He moved them inside the moccasins and decided that they were numb.

He pulled the mitten on hurriedly and stood up. He was a bit frightened. He stamped up and down until the stinging returned into the feet. It certainly was cold, was his thought. That man from Sulphur Creek had spoken the truth when telling how cold it sometimes got in the country. And he had laughed at him at the time! That showed one must not be too sure of things. There was no mistake about it, it *was* cold. He strode up and down, stamping his feet and threshing his arms, until reassured by the returning warmth. Then he got out matches and proceeded to make a fire. From the undergrowth, where high water of the previous spring had lodged a supply of seasoned twigs, he got his firewood. Working carefully from a small beginning, he soon had a roaring fire, over which he thawed the ice from his face and in the protection of which he ate his biscuits. For the moment the cold of space was outwitted. The dog took satisfaction in the fire, stretching out close enough for warmth and far enough away to escape being singed.

When the man had finished, he filled his pipe and took his comfortable time over a smoke. Then he pulled on his mittens, settled the ear-flaps of his cap firmly about his ears, and took the creek trail up the left fork. The dog was disappointed and yearned back towards the fire. This man did not know cold. Possibly all the generations of his ancestry had been ignorant of cold, of real cold, of cold one hundred and seven degrees below freezing point. But the dog knew; all its ancestry knew, and it had inherited the knowledge. And it knew that it was not good to walk abroad in such fearful cold. It was the time to lie snug in a hole in the snow and wait for a curtain of cloud to be drawn across the face of outer space whence this cold came. On the other hand, there was no keen intimacy between the dog and the man. The one was the toil slave of the other, and the only caresses it had ever received were the caresses of the whip lash and of harsh and menacing throat sounds that threatened the whip lash. So the dog made no effort to communicate its apprehension to the man. It was not concerned in the welfare of the man; it was for its own sake that it yearned back towards the fire. But the man whistled, and spoke to it with the sound of whip lashes, and the dog swung in at the man's heels and followed after.

The man took a chew of tobacco and proceeded to start a new amber beard. Also, his moist breath quickly powdered with white his moustache, eyebrows, and lashes. There did not seem to be so many springs on the left fork of the Henderson, and for half an hour the man saw no signs of any. And then it happened. At a place where there were no signs, where the soft, unbroken snow seemed to advertise solidity beneath, the man broke through. It was not deep. He wet himself half-way to the knees before he floundered out to the firm crust.

He was angry, and cursed his luck aloud. He had hoped to get into camp with the boys at six o'clock, and this would delay him an hour, for he would have to build a fire and dry out his footgear. This was imperative at that low temperature —he knew that much; and he turned aside to the bank, which he climbed. On top, tangled in the underbrush about the trunks of several small spruce trees, was a high-water deposit of dry firewood—sticks and twigs, principally, but also larger portions of seasoned branches and fine, dry, last year's grasses. He threw down several large pieces on top of the snow. This served for a foundation and prevented the young flame from drowning itself in the snow it otherwise would melt. The flame he got by touching a match to a small shred of birch bark that he took from his pocket. This burned even more readily than paper. Placing it on the foundation, he fed the young flame with wisps of dry grass and with the tiniest dry twigs.

He worked slowly and carefully, keenly aware of his danger. Gradually, as the flame grew stronger, he increased the size of the twigs with which he fed it. He squatted in the snow pulling the twigs out from their entanglement in the brush and feeding directly to the flame. He knew there must be no failure. When it is seventy-five below zero, a man must not fail in his first attempt to build a fire—that is, if his feet are wet. If his feet are dry, and he fails, he can run along the trail for half a mile and restore his circulation. But the circulation of wet and freezing feet cannot be restored by running when it is seventy-five below. No matter how fast he runs, the wet feet will freeze the harder.

All this the man knew. The old-timer on Sulphur Creek had told him about it the previous fall, and now he was appreciating the advice. Already all sensation had gone out of his feet. To build the fire he had been forced to remove his mittens, and the fingers had quickly gone numb. His pace of four miles an hour had kept his heart pumping blood to the surface of his body and to all the extremities. But the instant he stopped, the action of the pump eased down. The cold of space smote the unprotected tip of the planet, and he, being on that unprotected tip, received the full force of the blow. The blood of his body recoiled before it. The blood was alive, like the dog, and like the dog it wanted to hide away and cover itself up from the fearful cold. So long as he walked four miles an hour, he pumped that blood willy-nilly, to the surface; but now it ebbed away and sank down into the recesses of his body. The extremities were the first to feel its absence. His wet feet froze the faster, and his exposed fingers numbed the faster, though they had not yet begun to freeze. Nose and cheeks were already freezing, while the skin of all his body chilled as it lost its blood.

But he was safe. Toes and nose and cheeks would be only touched by the frost, for the fire was beginning to burn with strength. He was feeding it with twigs the size of his finger. In another minute he would be able to feed it with branches the size of his wrist, and then he could remove his wet footgear, and, while it dried, he could keep his naked feet warm by the fire, rubbing them at first, of course, with snow. The fire was a success. He was safe. He remembered the advice of the old-timer on Sulphur Creek, and smiled. The old-timer had been very serious in laying down the law that no man must travel alone in the Klondike after fifty below. Well, here he was; he had had the accident; he was alone; and he had saved himself. Those old-timers were rather womanish, some of them, he thought. All a man had to do was to keep his head, and he was all right. Any man who was a man could travel alone. But it was surprising, the rapidity with which his cheeks and nose were freezing. And he had not thought his fingers could go lifeless in so short a time. Lifeless they were, for he could scarcely make them move together to grip a twig, and they seemed remote from his body and from him. When he touched a twig, he had to look and see whether or not he had hold of it. The wires were pretty well down between him and his finger ends.

All of which counted for little. There was the fire, snapping and crackling and promising life with every dancing flame. He started to untie his moccasins. They were coated with ice; the thick German socks were like sheaths of iron halfway to the knees; and the moccasin strings were like rods of steel all twisted and knotted as by some conflagration. For a moment he tugged with his numb fingers, then, realizing the folly of it, he drew his sheath knife.

But before he could cut the strings, it happened. It was his own fault or, rather, his mistake. He should not have built the fire under the spruce tree. He should have built it in the open. But it had been easier to pull the twigs from the brush and drop them directly on the fire. Now the tree under which he had done this carried a weight of snow on its boughs. No wind had blown for weeks, and each bough was fully freighted. Each time he had pulled a twig he had communicated a slight agitation to the tree—an imperceptible agitation, so far as he was concerned, but an agitation sufficient to bring about the disaster. High up in the tree one bough capsized its load of snow. This fell on the boughs beneath, capsizing them. This process continued, spreading out and involving the whole tree. It grew like an avalanche, and it descended without warning upon the man and the fire, and the fire was blotted out! Where it had burned was a mantle of fresh and disordered snow.

The man was shocked. It was as though he had just heard his own sentence of death. For a moment he sat and stared at the spot where the fire had been. Then he grew very calm. Perhaps the old-timer on Sulphur Creek was right. If he had only had a trail mate he would have been in no danger now. The trail mate could have built the fire. Well, it was up to him to build the fire over again, and this second time there must be no failure. Even if he succeeded, he would most likely lose some toes. His feet must be badly frozen by now, and there would be some time before the second fire was ready.

Such were his thoughts, but he did not sit and think them. He was busy all the time they were passing through his mind. He made a new foundation for a fire, this time in the open, where no treacherous tree could blot it out. Next he gathered dry grasses and tiny twigs from the high-water flotsam. He could not bring his fingers together to pull them out, but he was able to gather them by the handful. In this way he got many rotten twigs and bits of green moss that were undesirable, but it was the best he could do. He worked methodically, even collecting an armful of the larger branches to be used later when the fire gathered strength. And all the while the dog sat and watched him, a certain yearning wistfulness in its eyes, for it looked upon him as the fire provider, and the fire was slow in coming.

When all was ready, the man reached in his pocket for a second piece of birch bark. He knew the bark was there, and, though he could not feel it with his fingers, he could hear its crisp rustling as he fumbled for it. Try as he would, he could not clutch hold of it. And all the time, in his consciousness, was the knowledge that each instant his feet were freezing. This thought tended to put him in a panic, but he fought against it and kept calm. He pulled on his mittens with his teeth, and threshed his arms back and forth, beating his hands with all his might against his sides. He did this sitting down, and he stood up to do it; and all the while the dog sat in the snow, its wolf brush of a tail curled around warmly over its forefront, its sharp wolf ears pricked forward intently as it watched the man. And the man, as he beat and threshed with his arms and hands, felt a great surge of envy as he regarded the creature that was warm and secure in its natural covering.

After a time he was aware of the first faraway signals of sensation in his beaten fingers. The faint tingling grew stronger till it evolved into a stinging ache that was excruciating, but which the man hailed with satisfaction. He stripped the mitten from his right hand and fetched forth the birch bark. The exposed fingers were quickly going numb again. Next he brought out his bunch of sulphur matches. But the tremendous cold had already driven the life out of his fingers. In his effort to separate one match from the others, the whole bunch fell in the snow. He tried to pick it out of the snow, but failed. The dead fingers could neither touch nor clutch. He was very careful. He drove the thought of his freezing feet, and nose, and cheeks, out of his mind, devoting his whole soul to the matches. He watched, using the sense of vision in place of that touch, and when he saw his fingers on each side the bunch, he closed them—that is, he willed to close them, for the wires were down, and the fingers did not obey. He pulled the mitten on the right hand, and beat it fiercely against his knee. Then with both mittened hands, he scooped the bunch of matches, along with much snow, into his lap. Yet he was no better off.

After some manipulation he managed to get the bunch between the heels of his mittened hands. In this fashion he carried it to his mouth. The ice crackled and snapped when by a violent effort he opened his mouth. He drew the lower jaw in, curled the upper lip out of the way, and scraped the bunch with his upper teeth in order to separate a match. He succeeded in getting one, which he dropped on his lap. He was no better off. He could not pick it up. Then he devised a way. He picked it up in his teeth and scratched it on his leg. Twenty times he scratched before he succeeded in lighting it. As it flamed he held it with his teeth to the birch bark. But the burning brimstone went up his nostrils and into his lungs, causing him to cough spasmodically. The match fell into the snow and went out.

The old-timer on Sulphur Creek was right, he thought in the moment of controlled despair that ensued: after fifty below, a man should travel with a partner. He beat his hands, but failed in exciting any sensation. Suddenly he bared both hands, removing the mittens with his teeth. He caught the whole bunch between the heels of his hands. His arm muscles not being frozen enabled him to press the hand heels tightly against the matches. Then he scratched the bunch along his leg. It flared into flame, seventy sulphur matches at once! There was no wind to blow them out. He kept his head to one side to escape the strangling fumes, and held the blazing bunch to the birch bark. As he so held it, he became aware of sensation in his hand. His flesh was burning. He could smell it. Deep down below the surface he could feel it. The sensation developed into pain that grew acute. And still he endured it, holding the flame of the matches clumsily to the bark that would not light readily because his own burning hands were in the way, absorbing most of the flame.

At last, when he could endure no more, he jerked his hands apart. The blazing matches fell sizzling into the snow, but the birch bark was alight. He began laying dry grasses and the tiniest twigs on the flame. He could not pick and choose, for he had to lift the fuel between the heels of his hands. Small pieces of rotten wood and green moss clung to the twigs, and he bit them off as well as he could with his teeth. He cherished the flame carefully and awkwardly. It meant life, and it must not perish. The withdrawal of blood from the surface of his body now made him begin to shiver, and he grew more awkward. A large piece of green moss fell squarely on the little fire. He tried to poke it out with his fingers, but his shivering frame made him poke too far, and he disrupted the nucleus of the little fire, the burning grasses and tiny twigs separating and scattering. He tried to poke them together again, but in spite of the tenseness of the effort, his shivering got away with him, and the twigs were hopelessly scattered. Each twig gushed a puff of smoke and went out. The fire provider had failed. As he looked apathetically about him, his eyes chanced on the dog, sitting across the ruins of the fire from him, in the snow, making restless, hunching movements, slightly lifting one forefoot and then the other, shifting its weight back and forth on them with wistful eagerness.

The sight of the dog put a wild idea into his head. He remembered the tale of the man, caught in a blizzard, who killed a steer and crawled inside the carcass, and so was saved. He would kill the dog and bury his hands in the warm body until the numbness went out of them. Then he could build another fire. He spoke to the dog, calling it to him; but in his voice was a strange note of fear that frightened the animal, who had never known the man to speak in such a way before. Something was the matter, and its suspicious nature sensed danger—it knew not what danger, but somewhere, somehow, in its brain arose an apprehension of the man. It flattened its ears down at the sound of the man's voice, and its restless, hunching movements and the liftings and shiftings of its forefeet became more pronounced; but it would not come to the man. He got on his hands and knees and crawled towards the dog. This unusual posture again excited suspicion, and the animal sidled mincingly away.

The man sat up in the snow for a moment and struggled for calmness. Then he pulled on his mittens, by means of his teeth, and got upon his feet. He glanced down at first in order to assure himself that he was really standing up, for the absence of sensation in his feet left him unrelated to the earth. His erect position in itself started to drive the webs of suspicion from the dog's mind; and when he spoke peremptorily, with the sound of whip lashes in his voice, the dog rendered its customary allegiance and came to him. As it came within reaching distance, the man lost his control. His arms flashed out to the dog, and he experienced genuine surprise when he discovered that his hands could not clutch, that there was neither bend nor feeling in the fingers. He had forgotten for the moment that they were frozen and that they were freezing more and more. All this happened quickly, and before the animal could get away, he encircled its body with his arms. He sat down in the snow, and in this fashion held the dog, while it snarled and whined and struggled.

But it was all he could do, hold its body encircled in his arms and sit there. He realized he could not kill the dog. There was no way to do it. With his helpless hands he could neither draw nor hold his sheath knife nor throttle the animal. He released it, and it plunged wildly away, with tail between its legs, and still snarling. It halted forty feet away and surveyed him curiously, with ears sharply pricked forward.

The man looked down at his hands in order to locate them, and found them hanging on the ends of his arms. It struck him as curious that one should have to use his eyes in order to find out where his hands were. He began threshing his arms back and forth, beating the mittened hands against his sides. He did this for five minutes, violently, and his heart pumped enough blood up to the surface to put a stop to his shivering. But no sensation was aroused in the hands. He had an impression that they hung like weights on the ends of his arms, but when he tried to run the impression down, he could not find it.

A certain fear of death, dull and oppressive, came to him. This fear quickly became poignant as he realized that it was no longer a mere matter of freezing his fingers and toes, or of losing his hands and feet, but that it was a matter of life and death with the chances against him. This threw him into a panic, and he turned and ran up the creek bed along the old, dim trail. The dog joined in behind him and kept up with him. He ran blindly, without intention, in fear such as he had never known in his life. Slowly, as he ploughed and floundered through the snow, he began to see things again—the banks of the creek, the old timber jams, the leafless aspens, and the sky. The running made him feel better. He did not shiver. Maybe, if he ran on, his feet would thaw out; and, anyway, if he ran far enough, he would reach camp and the boys. Without doubt he would lose some fingers and toes and some of his face; but the boys would take care of him, and save the rest of him when he got there. And at the same time there was another thought in his mind that said he would never get to the camp and the boys; that it was too many miles away, that the freezing had too great a start on him, and that he would soon be stiff and dead. This thought he kept in the background and refused to consider. Sometimes it pushed itself forward and demanded to be heard, but he thrust it back and strove to think of other things.

It struck him as curious that he could run at all on feet so frozen that he could not feel them when they struck the earth and took the weight of his body. He seemed to himself to skim along above the surface, and to have no connection with the earth. Somewhere he had once seen a winged Mercury, and he wondered if Mercury felt as he felt when skimming over the earth.

His theory of running until he reached camp and the boys had one flaw in it: he lacked the endurance. Several times he stumbled, and finally he tottered, crumpled up, and fell. When he tried to rise, he failed. He must sit and rest, he decided, and next time he would merely walk and keep on going. As he sat and regained his breath, he noted that he was feeling quite warm and comfortable. He was not shivering, and it even seemed that a warm glow had come to his chest and trunk. And yet, when he touched his nose or cheeks, there was no sensation. Running would not thaw them out. Nor would it thaw out his hands and feet. Then the thought came to him that the frozen portions of his body must be extending. He tried to keep this thought down, to forget it, to think of something else; he was aware of the panicky feeling that it caused, and he was afraid of the panic. But the thought asserted itself, and persisted, until it produced a vision of his body totally frozen. This was too much, and he made another wild run along the trail. Once he slowed down to a walk, but the thought of the freezing extending itself made him run again.

And all the time the dog ran with him, at his heels. When he fell down a second time, it curled its tail over its forefeet and sat in front of him, facing him, curiously eager and intent. The warmth and security of the animal angered him, and he cursed it till it flattened down its ears appeasingly. This time the shivering came more quickly upon the man. He was losing in his battle with the frost. It was creeping into his body from all sides. The thought of it drove him on, but he ran no more than a hundred feet, when he staggered and pitched headlong. It was his last panic. When he had recovered his breath and control, he sat up and entertained in his mind the conception of meeting death with dignity. However, the conception did not come to him in such terms. His idea of it was that he had been making a fool of himself, running around like a chicken with its head cut off—such was the simile that occurred to him. Well, he was bound to freeze anyway, and he might as well take it decently. With this new-found peace of mind came the first glimmerings of drowsiness. A good idea, he thought, to sleep off to death. It was like taking an anaesthetic. Freezing was not so bad as people thought. There were lots worse ways to die.

He pictured the boys finding his body next day. Suddenly he found himself with them, coming along the trail looking for himself. And, still with them, he came around a turn in the trail and found himself lying in the snow. He did not belong with himself any more, for even then he was out of himself, standing with the boys and looking at himself in the snow. It certainly was cold, was his thought. When he got back to the States he could tell the folks what real cold was. He drifted on from this to a vision of the old-timer on Sulphur Creek. He could see him quite clearly, warm and comfortable, and smoking a pipe.

'You were right, old hoss; you were right,' the man mumbled to the old-timer of Sulphur Creek.

Then the man drowsed off into what seemed to him the most comfortable and satisfying sleep he had ever known. The dog sat facing him and waiting. The brief day drew to a close in a long, slow twilight. There were no signs of a fire to be made, and, besides, never in the dog's experience had it known a man to sit like that in the snow and make no fire. As the twilight drew on, its eager yearning for the fire mastered it, and with a great lifting and shifting of forefeet, it whined softly, then flattened its ears down in anticipation of being chidden by the man. But the man remained silent. Later the dog whined loudly. And still later it crept close to the man and caught the scent of death. This made the animal bristle and back away. A little longer it delayed, howling under the stars that leaped and danced and shone brightly in the cold sky. Then it turned and trotted up the trail in the direction of the camp it knew, where were the other food providers and fire providers.

The Law of Life

Old Koskoosh listened greedily. Though his sight had long since faded, his hearing was still acute, and the slightest sound penetrated to the glimmering intelligence which yet abode behind the withered forehead, but which no longer gazed forth upon the things of the world. Ah! that was Sit-cum-to-ha, shrilly anathematizing the dogs, as she cuffed and beat them into the harnesses. Sit-cum-to-ha was his daughter's daughter, but she was too busy to waste a thought upon her broken grandfather, sitting alone there in the snow, forlorn and helpless. Camp must be broken. The long trail waited while the short day refused to linger. Life called her, and the duties of life, not death. And he was very close to death now.

The thought made the old man panicky for the moment, and he stretched forth a palsied hand which wandered tremblingly over the small heap of dry wood beside him. Reassured that it was indeed there, his hand returned to the shelter of his mangy furs, and he again fell to listening. The sulky crackling of half-frozen hides told him that the chief's moose-skin lodge had been struck, and even then was being rammed and jammed into portable compass. The chief was his son, stalwart and strong, head man of the tribesmen, and a mighty hunter. As the women toiled with the camp luggage, his voice rose, chiding them for their slowness. Old Koskoosh strained his ears. It was the last time he would hear that voice. There went Geehow's lodge! And Tusken's! Seven, eight, nine; only the shaman's could be still standing. There! They were at work upon it now. He could hear the shaman grunt as he piled it on the sled. A child whimpered, and a woman soothed it with soft, crooning gutturals. Little Koo-tee, the old man thought, a fretful child, and not overstrong. It would die soon, perhaps, and they would burn a hole through the frozen tundra and pile rocks above to keep the wolverines away. Well, what did it matter? A few years at best, and as many an empty belly as a full one. And in the end, Death waited, ever-hungry and hungriest of them all.

What was that? Oh, the men lashing the sleds and drawing tight the thongs. He listened, who would listen no more. The whip-lashes snarled and bit among the dogs. Hear them whine! How they hated the work and the trail! They were off! Sled after sled churned slowly away into the silence. They were gone. They had passed out of his life, and he faced the last bitter hour alone. No. The snow crunched beneath a moccasin; a man stood beside him; upon his head a hand rested gently. His son was good to do this thing. He remembered other old men whose sons had not waited after the tribe. But his son had. He wandered away into the past, till the young man's voice brought him back.

'Is it well with you?' he asked.

And the old man answered, 'It is well.'

'There be wood beside you,' the younger man continued, 'and the fire burns bright. The morning is grey, and the cold has broken. It will snow presently. Even now it is snowing.'

'Ay, even now it is snowing.'

'The tribesmen hurry. Their bales are heavy and their bellies flat with lack of feasting. The trail is long and they travel fast. I go now. It is well?'

'It is well. I am as a last year's leaf, clinging lightly to the stem. The first breath that blows, and I fall. My voice is become like an old woman's. My eyes no longer show me the way of my feet, and my feet are heavy, and I am tired. It is well.'

He bowed his head in content till the last noise of the complaining snow had died away, and he knew his son was beyond recall. Then his hand crept out in haste to the wood. It alone stood betwixt him and the eternity that yawned in upon him. At last the measure of his life was a handful of faggots. One by one they would go to feed the fire, and just so, step by step, death would creep upon him. When the last stick had surrendered up its heat, the frost would begin to gather strength.

First his feet would yield, then his hands; and the numbness would travel, slowly, from the extremities to the body. His head would fall forward upon his knees, and he would rest. It was easy. All men must die.

He did not complain. It was the way of life, and it was just. He had been born close to the earth, close to the earth had he lived, and the law thereof was not new to him. It was the law of all flesh. Nature was not kindly to the flesh. She had no concern for that concrete thing called the individual. Her interest lay in the species, the race. This was the deepest abstraction old Koskoosh's barbaric mind was capable of, but he grasped it firmly. He saw it exemplified in all life. The rise of the sap, the bursting greenness of the willow bud. The fall of the yellow leaf—in this alone was told the whole history. But one task did Nature set the individual. Did he not perform it, he died. Did he perform it, it was all the same, he died. Nature did not care; there were plenty who were obedient, and it was only the obedience in this matter, not the obedient, which lived and lived always. The tribe of Koskoosh was very old. The old men he had known when a boy, had known old men before them. Therefore it was true that the tribe lived, that it stood for the obedience of all its members, way down into the forgotten past, whose very resting-places were unremembered. They did not count; they were episodes. They had passed away like clouds from a summer sky. He also was an episode, and would pass away. Nature did not care. To life she set one task, gave one law. To perpetuate was the task of life, its law was death. A maiden was a good creature to look upon, full-breasted and strong, with spring to her step and light in her eyes. But her task was yet before her. The light in her eyes brightened, her step quickened, she was now bold with the young men, now timid, and she gave them of her own unrest. And ever she grew fairer and yet fairer to look upon, till some hunter, able no longer to withhold himself, took her to his lodge to cook and toil for him and to become the mother of his children. And with the coming of her offspring her looks left her. Her limbs dragged and shuffled, her eyes dimmed and bleared, and only the little children found joy against the withered cheek of the old squaw by the fire. Her task was done. But a little while, on the first pinch of famine or the first long trail, and she would be left, even as he had been left, in the snow, with a little pile of wood. Such was the law.

He placed a stick carefully upon the fire and resumed his meditations. It was the same everywhere, with all things. The mosquitoes vanished with the first frost. The little tree-squirrel crawled away to die. When age settled upon the rabbit it became slow and heavy, and could no longer out-foot its enemies. Even the big bald-face grew clumsy and blind and quarrelsome, in the end to be dragged down by a handful of yelping huskies. He remembered how he had abandoned his own father on an upper reach of the Klondyke one winter, the the winter before the missionary came with his talk-books and his box of medicines. Many a time had Koskoosh smacked his lips over the recollection of that box, though now his mouth refused to moisten. The 'pain-killer' had been especially good. But the missionary was a bother after all, for he brought no meat into the camp, and he ate heartily, and the hunters grumbled. But he chilled his lungs on the divide by the Mayo, and the dogs afterwards nosed the stones away and fought over his bones.

Koskoosh placed another stick on the fire and harked back deeper into the past. There was the time of the Great Famine, when the old men crouched empty-bellied to the fire, and let fall from their lips dim traditions of the ancient day when the Yukon ran wide open for three winters, and then lay frozen for three summers. He had lost his mother in that famine. In the summer the salmon run had failed, and the tribe looked forward to the winter and the coming of the caribou. Then the winter came, but with it there were no caribou. Never had the like been known, not even in the lives of the old men. But the caribou did not come, and it was the seventh year, and the rabbits had not replenished, and the dogs were naught but bundles of bones. And through the long darkness the children wailed and died, and the women, and the old men; and not one in ten of the tribe lived to meet the sun when it came back in the spring. That *was* a famine!

But he had seen times of plenty, too, when the meat spoiled on their hands, and the dogs were fat and worthless with over-eating—times when they let the game go unkilled, and the women were fertile, and the lodges were cluttered with sprawl-ling, men-children and women-children. Then it was the men became high-stomached, and revived ancient quarrels, and crossed the divides to the south to kill the Pellys, and to the west that they might sit by the dead fires of the Tananas. He remembered, when a boy, during a time of plenty, when he saw a moose pulled down by the wolves. Zing-ha lay with him in the snow and watched—Zing-ha, who later became the craftiest of hunters, and who, in the end, fell through an air-hole on the Yukon. They found him, a month afterward, just as he had crawled halfway out and frozen stiff to the ice.

But the moose. Zing-ha and he had gone out that day to play at hunting after the manner of their fathers. On the bed of the creek they struck the fresh track of a moose, and with it the tracks of many wolves. 'An old one,' Zing-ha, who was quicker at reading the sign, said—'an old one who cannot keep up with the herd. The wolves have cut him out from his brothers, and they will never leave him.' And it was so. It was their way. By day and by night, never resting, snarling on his heels, snapping at his nose, they would stay by him to the end. How Zing-ha and he felt the blood-lust quicken! The finish would be a sight to see!

Eager-footed, they took the trail, and even he, Koskoosh, slow of sight and an unversed tracker, could have followed it blind, it was so wide. Hot were they on the heels of the chase, reading the grim tragedy, fresh-written, at every step. Now they came to where the moose had made a stand. Thrice the length of a grown man's body, in every direction, had the snow been stamped about and uptossed. In the midst were the deep impressions of the splay-hoofed game, and all about, everywhere, were the lighter footmarks of the wolves. Some, while their brothers harried the kill, had lain to one side and rested. The full-stretch impress of their bodies in the snow was as perfect as though made the moment before. One wolf had been caught in a wild lunge of the maddened victim and trampled to death. A few bones, well picked, bore witness.

Again, they ceased the uplift of their snowshoes at a second stand. Here the great animal had fought desperately. Twice had he been dragged down, as the snow attested, and twice had he shaken his assailants clear and gained footing once more. He had done his task long since, but none the less was life dear to him. Zing-ha said it was a strange thing, a moose once down to get free again; but this one certainly had. The shaman would see signs and wonders in this when they told him.

And yet again, they came to where the moose had made to mount the bank and gain the timber. But his foes had laid on from behind, till he reared and fell back upon them, crushing two deep into the snow. It was plain the kill was at hand, for their brothers had left them untouched. Two more stands were hurried past, brief in time-length and very close together. The trail was red now, and the clean stride of the great beast had grown short and slovenly. Then they heard the first sounds of the battle—not the full-throated chorus of the chase, but the short, snappy bark which spoke of close quarters and teeth to flesh. Crawling up the wind, Zing-ha bellied it through the snow, and with him crept he, Koskoosh, who was to be chief of the tribesmen in the years to come. Together they shoved aside the under branches of a young spruce and peered forth. It was the end they saw.

The picture, like all of youth's impressions, was still strong with him, and his dim eyes watched the end played out as vividly as in that far-off time. Koskoosh marvelled at this, for in the days which followed, when he was a leader of men and a head of councillors, he had done great deeds and made his name a curse in the mouths of the Pellys, to say naught of the strange white man he had killed, knife to knife, in open fight.

For long he pondered on the days of his youth, till the fire died down and the frost bit deeper. He replenished it with two sticks this time, and gauged his grip on life by what remained. If Sit-cum-to-ha had only remembered her grandfather, and gathered a larger armful, his hours would have been longer. It would have been easy. But she was ever a careless child, and honoured not her ancestors from the time the Beaver, son of the son of Zing-ha, first cast eyes upon her. Well, what mattered it? Had he not done likewise in his own quick youth? For a while he listened to the silence. Perhaps the heart of his son might soften, and he would come back with the dogs to take his old father on with the tribe to where the caribou ran thick and the fat hung heavy upon them.

He strained his ears, his restless brain for the moment stilled. Not a stir, nothing. He alone took breath in the midst of the great silence. It was very lonely. Hark! What was that? A chill passed over his body. The familiar, long-drawn howl broke the void, and it was close at hand. Then on his darkened eyes was projected the vision of the moose—the old bull moose —the torn flanks and bloody sides, the riddled mane, and the great branching horns, down low and tossing to the last. He saw the flashing forms of grey, the gleaming eyes, the lolling tongues, the slavered fangs. And he saw the inexorable circle close in till it became a dark point in the midst of the stamped snow.

A cold muzzle thrust against his cheek, and at its touch his soul leaped back to the present. His hand shot into the fire and dragged out a burning faggot. Overcome for the nonce by his hereditary fear of man, the brute retreated, raising a prolonged call to his brothers; and greedily they answered, till a ring of crouching, jaw-slobbered grey was stretched round about. The old man listened to the drawing in of this circle. He waved his brand wildly, and sniffs turned to snarls; but the panting brutes refused to scatter. Now one wormed his chest forward, dragging his haunches after, now a second, now a third; but never a one drew back. Why should he cling to life? he asked, and dropped the blazing stick into the snow. It sizzled and went out. The circle grunted uneasily, but held its own. Again he saw the last stand of the old bull moose, and Koskoosh dropped his head wearily upon his knees. What did it matter after all? Was it not the law of life?

The Apostate

'Now I wake me up to work;
I pray the Lord I may not shirk.
If I should die before the night,
I pray the Lord my work's all right.
Amen.'

'If you don't git up, Johnny, I won't give you a bite to eat!'

The threat had no effect on the boy. He clung stubbornly to sleep, fighting for its oblivion as the dreamer fights for his dream. The boy's hands loosely clenched themselves, and he made feeble, spasmodic blows at the air. These blows were intended for his mother, but she betrayed practised familiarity in avoiding them as she shook him roughly by the shoulder.

'Lemme 'lone!'

It was a cry that began, muffled, in the deeps of sleep, that swiftly rushed upward, like a wail, into passionate belligerence, and that died away, and sank down into an inarticulate whine. It was a bestial cry, as of a soul in torment, filled with infinite protest and pain.

But she did not mind. She was a sad-eyed, tired-faced woman, and she had grown used to this task, which she repeated every day of her life. She got a grip on the bed-clothes and tried to strip them down; but the boy, ceasing his punching clung to them desperately. In a huddle, at the foot of the bed, he still remained covered. Then she tried dragging the bedding to the floor. The boy opposed her. She braced herself. Hers was the superior weight, and the boy and bedding gave, the former instinctively following the latter in order to shelter against the chill of the room that bit into his body.

As he toppled on the edge of the bed it seemed that he must

fall head-first to the floor. But consciousness fluttered up in him. He righted himself and for a moment perilously balanced. Then he struck the floor on his feet. On the instant his mother seized him by the shoulders and shook him. Again his fists struck out, this time with more force and directness. At the same time his eyes opened. She released him. He was awake.

'All right,' he mumbled.

She caught up the lamp and hurried out, leaving him in darkness.

'You'll be docked,' she warned back to him.

He did not mind the darkness. When he had got into his clothes he went out into the kitchen. His tread was very heavy for so thin and light a boy. His legs dragged with their own weight, which seemed unreasonable because they were such skinny legs. He drew a broken-bottomed chair to the table.

'Johnny!' his mother called sharply.

He arose as sharply from the chair, and, without a word, went to the sink. It was a greasy, filthy sink. A smell came up from the outlet. He took no notice of it. That a sink should smell was to him part of the natural order, just as it was a part of the natural order that the soap should be grimy with dishwater and hard to lather. Nor did he try very hard to make it lather. Several splashes of the cold water from the running faucet completed the function. He did not wash his teeth. For that matter he had never seen a toothbrush, nor did he know that there existed beings in the world who were guilty of so great a foolishness as tooth-washing.

'You might wash yourself wunst a day without bein' told,' his mother complained.

She was holding a broken lid on the pot as she poured two cups of coffee. He made no remark, for this was a standing quarrel between them, and the one thing upon which his mother was hard as adamant. 'Wunst' a day it was compulsory that he should wash his face. He dried himself on a greasy towel, damp and dirty and ragged, that left his face covered with shreds of lint.

'I wish we didn't live so far away,' she said, as he sat down. 'I try to do the best I can. You know that. But a dollar on the rent is such a savin', an' we've more room here. You know that.'

He scarcely followed her. He had heard it all before, many times. The range of her thought was limited, and she was ever harking back to the hardship worked upon them by living so far from the mills.

'A dollar means more grub,' he remarked sententiously. 'I'd sooner do the walkin' an' git the grub.'

He ate hurriedly, half-chewing the bread and washing the unmasticated chunks down with coffee. The hot and muddy liquid went by the name of coffee. Johnny thought it was coffee—and excellent coffee. That was one of the few illusions that remained to him. He had never drunk real coffee in his life.

In addition to the bread, there was a small piece of cold pork. His mother refilled his cup with coffee. As he was finishing the bread, he began to watch if more was forthcoming. She intercepted his questioning glance.

'Now, don't be hoggish, Johnny,' was her comment. 'You've had your share. You brothers an' sisters are smaller'n you.'

He did not answer the rebuke. He was not much of a talker. Also, he ceased his hungry glancing for more. He was uncomplaining, with a patience that was as terrible as the school in which it had been learned. He finished his coffee, wiped his mouth on the back of his hand, and started to rise.

'Wait a second,' she said hastily. 'I guess the loaf kin stand you another slice—a thin 'un.'

There was a legerdemain in her actions. With all the seeming of cutting a slice from the loaf for him, she put loaf and slice back in the bread box and conveyed to him one of her own two slices. She believed she had deceived him, but he had noted her sleight-of-hand. Nevertheless, he took the bread shamelessly. He had a philosophy that his mother, because of her chronic sickliness, was not much of an eater anyway.

She saw that he was chewing the bread dry, and reached over and emptied her coffee cup into his.

'Don't set good somehow on my stomach this morning,' she explained.

A distant whistle, prolonged and shrieking, brought both of them to their feet. She glanced at the tin alarm-clock on the shelf. The hands stood at half-past five. The rest of the factory world was just arousing from sleep. She drew a shawl about her shoulders, and on her head put a dingy hat, shapeless and ancient.

'We've got to run,' she said, turning the wick of the lamp and blowing down the chimney.

They groped their way out and down the stairs. It was clear and cold, and Johnny shivered at the first contact with the outside air. The stars had not yet begun to pale in the sky, and the city lay in blackness. Both Johnny and his mother shuffled their feet as they walked. There was no ambition in the leg muscles to swing the feet clear of the ground.

After fifteen silent minutes, his mother turned off to the right.

'Don't be late,' was her final warning from out of the dark that was swallowing her up.

He made no response, steadily keeping on his way. In the factory quarter, doors were opening everywhere, and he was soon one of a multitude that pressed onward through the dark. As he entered the factory gate the whistle blew again. He glanced at the east. Across a ragged sky-line of housetops a pale light was beginning to creep. This much he saw of the days as he turned his back upon it and joined his work gang.

He took his place in one of many long rows of machines. Before him, above a bin filled with small bobbins, were large bobbins revolving rapidly. Upon these he wound the jute-twine of the small bobbins. The work was simple. All that was required was celerity. The small bobbins were emptied so rapidly and there were so many large bobbins that did the emptying, that there were no idle moments.

He worked mechanically. When a small bobbin ran out, he used his left hand for a brake, stopping the large bobbin and at the same time, with thumb and forefinger, catching the flying end of twine. Also, at the same time, with his right hand, he caught up the loose twine-end of a small bobbin. These various acts with both hands were performed simultaneously and swiftly. Then there would come a flash of his hands as he looped the weaver's knot and released the bobbin. There was nothing difficult about weavers' knots. He once boasted he could tie them in his sleep. And for that matter, he sometimes did, toiling centuries long in a single night at tying an endless succession of weavers' knots.

Some of the boys shirked, wasting time and machinery by not replacing the small bobbins when they ran out. And there was an overseer to prevent this. He caught Johnny's neighbour at the trick, and boxed his ears.

'Look at Johnny there—why ain't you like him?' the overseer wrathfully demanded.

Johnny's bobbins were running full blast, but he did not thrill at the indirect praise. There had been a time . . . but that was long ago, very long ago. His apathetic face was expressionless as he listened to himself being held up as a shining example. He was the perfect worker. He knew that. He had been told so, often. It was a commonplace, and besides it didn't seem to mean anything to him any more. From the perfect worker he had evolved into the perfect machine. When his work went wrong, it was with him as with the machine, due to faulty material. It would have been as possible for a perfect nail-die to cut imperfect nails as for him to make a mistake.

And small wonder. There had never been a time when he had not been in intimate relationship with machines. Machinery had almost been bred into him, and at any rate he had been brought up on it. Twelve years before, there had been a small flutter of excitement in the loom room of this very mill. Johnny's mother had fainted. They stretched her out on the floor in the midst of the shrieking machines. A couple of elderly women were called from their looms. The foreman assisted. And in a few minutes there was one more soul in the loom room than had entered by the doors. It was Johnny, born with the pounding, crashing roar of the looms in his ears, drawing with his first breath the warm, moist air that was thick with flying lint. He had coughed that first day in order to rid his lungs of the lint; and for the same reason he had coughed ever since.

The boy alongside of Johnny whimpered and sniffed. The boy's face was convulsed with hatred for the overseer who kept a threatening eye on him from a distance; but every bobbin was running full. The boy yelled terrible oaths into the whirling bobbins before him; but the sound did not carry half a dozen feet, the roaring of the room holding it in and containing it like a wall.

Of all this Johnny took no notice. He had a way of accepting things. Besides, things grow monotonous by repetition, and this particular happening he had witnessed many times. It seemed to him as useless to oppose the overseer as to defy the will of a machine. Machines were made to go in certain ways and perform certain tasks. It was the same with the overseer.

But at eleven o'clock there was excitement in the room. In an apparently occult way the excitement instantly permeated everywhere. The one-legged boy who worked on the other side of Johnny bobbed swiftly across the floor to a bin truck that stood empty. Into this he dived out of sight, crutch and all. The superintendent of the mill was coming along, accompanied by a young man. He was well-dressed and wore a starched shirt—a gentleman in Johnny's classification of men, and also, the 'Inspector'.

He looked sharply at the boys as he passed along. Sometimes he stopped and asked questions. When he did so, he was compelled to shout at the top of his lungs, at which moments his face was ludicrously contorted with the strain of making himself heard. His quick eye noted the empty machine alongside of Johnny's, but he said nothing. Johnny also caught his eye, and he stopped abruptly. He caught Johnny by the arm to draw him back a step from the machine; but with an exclamation of surprise he released the arm.

'Pretty skinny,' the superintendent laughed anxiously.

'Pipe stems,' was the answer. 'Look at those legs. The boy's got the rickets—incipient, but he's got them. If epilepsy doesn't get him in the end, it will be because tuberculosis gets him first.'

Johnny listened, but did not understand. Furthermore he was not interested in future ills. There was an immediate and more serious ill that threatened him in the form of the inspector.

'Now, my boy, I want you to tell me the truth,' the inspector said, or shouted, bending close to the boy's ear to make him hear. 'How old are you?'

'Fourteen,' Johnny lied, and he lied with the full force of his lungs. So loudly did he lie that it started him off in a dry, hacking cough that lifted the lint which had been settling in his lungs all morning.

'Looks sixteen at least,' said the superintendent.

'Or sixty,' snapped the inspector.

'He's always looked that way.'

'How long?' asked the inspector, quickly.

'For years. Never gets a bit older.'

'Or younger, I dare say. I suppose he's worked here all these years?'

'Off and on—but that was before the new law was passed,' the superintendent hastened to add.

'Machine idle?' the inspector asked, pointing at the unoccupied machine beside Johnny's, in which the part-filled bobbins were flying like mad.

'Looks that way.' The superintendent motioned the overseer to him and shouted in his ear and pointed at the machine. 'Machine's idle,' he reported back to the inspector.

They passed on, and Johnny returned to his work, relieved in that the ill had been averted. But the one-legged boy was not so fortunate. The sharp-eyed inspector hauled him out at arm's length from the bin truck. His lips were quivering, and his face had all the expression of one upon whom was fallen profound and irremediable disaster. The overseer looked astounded, as though for the first time he had laid eyes on the boy, while the superintendent's face expressed shock and displeasure.

'I know him,' the inspector said. 'He's twelve years old. I've had him discharged from three factories inside the year. This makes the fourth.'

He turned to the one-legged boy. 'You promised me, word and honour, that you'd go to school.'

The one-legged boy burst into tears. 'Please, Mr. Inspector, two babies died on us, and we're awful poor.'

'What makes you cough that way?' the inspector demanded, as though charging him with crime.

And as in denial of guilt, the one legged-boy replied: 'It ain't nothin'. I jes' caught a cold last week, Mr. Inspector, that's all.'

In the end the one-legged boy went out of the room with the inspector, the latter accompanied by the anxious and protesting superintendent. After that monotony settled down again. The long morning and the longer afternoon wore away and the whistle blew for quitting time. Darkness had already fallen when Johnny passed out through the factory gate. In the interval the sun had made a golden ladder of the sky, flooded the world with its gracious warmth, and dropped down and disappeared in the west behind a ragged sky-line of house-tops.

Supper was the family meal of the day—the one meal at which Johnny encountered his younger brothers and sisters. It partook of the nature of an encounter, to him, for he was very old, while they were distressingly young. He had no patience with their excessive and amazing juvenility. He did not understand it. His own childhood was too far behind him. He was like an old and irritable man, annoyed by the turbulence of their young spirits that was to him arrant silliness. He glowered silently over his food, finding compensation in the thought that they would soon have to go to work. That would take the edge off them and make them sedate and dignified—like him. Thus it was, after the fashion of the human, that Johnny made himself a yard-stick with which to measure the universe.

During the meal, his mother explained in various ways and with infinite repetition that she was trying to do the best she could; so that it was with relief the scant meal ended, that Johnny shoved back his chair and arose. He debated for a moment between bed and the front door, and finally went out the latter. He did not go far. He sat down on the stoop, his knees drawn up and his narrow shoulders drooping forward, his elbows on his knees and the palms of his hands supporting his chin.

As he sat there, he did no thinking. He was just resting. So far as his mind was concerned it was asleep. His brothers and sisters came out, and with other children played noisily about him. An electric globe at the corner lighted their frolics. He was peevish and irritable, that they knew; but the spirit of adventure lured them into teasing him. They joined hands before him, and, keeping time with their bodies, chanted in his face weird and uncomplimentary doggerel. At first he snarled curses at them—curses he had learned from the lips of various foremen. Finding this futile, and remembering his dignity, he relapsed into dogged silence.

His brother Will, next to him in age, having just passed his tenth birthday, was the ring-leader. Johnny did not possess particularly kindly feelings towards him. His life had early been embittered by continual giving over and giving way to Will. He had a definite feeling that Will was greatly in his debt and was ungrateful about it. In his own playtime, far back in the dim past, he had been robbed of a large part of that playtime by being compelled to take care of Will. Will was a baby then, and then, as now, their mother had spent her days in the mills. To Johnny had fallen the part of little father and little mother as well.

Will seemed to show the benefit of the giving over and the giving way. He was well-built, fairly rugged, as tall as his elder brother and even heavier. It was as though the life-blood of the one had been diverted into the other's veins. And in spirits it was the same. Johnny was jaded, worn out, without resilience, while his younger brother seemed bursting and spilling over with exuberance.

The mocking chant rose louder and louder. Will leaned close as he danced, thrusting out his tongue. Johnny's left arm shot out and caught the other around the neck. At the same time he rapped his bony fist to the other's nose. It was a pathetically bony fist, but that it was sharp to hurt was evident by the squeal of pain it produced. The other children were uttering frightened cries, while Johnny's sister, Jennie, had dashed into the house.

He thrust Will from him, kicked him savagely on the shins, then reached for him and slammed him face downward in the dirt. Nor did he release him till the face had been rubbed into the dirt several times. Then the mother arrived, an anaemic whirlwind of solicitude and maternal wrath.

'Why can't he leave me alone?' was Johnny's reply to her up-braiding. 'Can't he see I'm tired?'

'I'm as big as you,' Will raged in her arms, his face a mass of tears, dirt, and blood. 'I'm as big as you now, an' I'm goin' to git bigger. Then I'll lick you—see if I don't.'

'You ought to be to work, seein' how big you are,' Johnny snarled. 'That's what's the matter with you. You ought to be to work. An' it's up to your ma to put you to work.'

'But he's too young,' she protested. 'He's only a little boy.'

'I was younger'n him when I started to work.'

Johnny's mouth was open, further to express the sense of unfairness that he felt, but the mouth closed with a snap. He turned gloomily on his heel and stalked into the house and to bed. The door of his room was open to let in warmth from the kitchen. As he undressed in the semi-darkness he could hear his mother talking with a neighbour woman who had dropped in. His mother was crying, and her speech was punctuated with spiritless sniffles.

'I can't make out what's gittin' into Johnny,' he could hear her say. 'He didn't used to be this way. He was a patient little angel.

'An' he *is* a good boy,' she hastened to defend. 'He's worked faithful, an' he did go to work too young. But it wasn't my fault. I do the best I can, I'm sure.'

Prolonged sniffling from the kitchen, and Johnny murmured to himself as his eyelids closed down, 'You betcher life I've worked faithful.'

The next morning he was torn bodily by his mother from the grip of sleep. Then came the meagre breakfast, the tramp through the dark, and the pale glimpse of day across the housetops as he turned his back on it and went in through the factory gate. It was another day, of all the days, and all the days were alike.

And yet there had been variety in his life—at the times he changed from one job to another, or was taken sick. When he was six, he was little mother and father to Will and the other children still younger. At seven he went into the mills—winding bobbins. When he was eight, he got work in another mill. His new job was marvellously easy. All he had to do was to sit down with a little stick in his hand and guide a stream of cloth that flowed past him. This stream of cloth came out of the maw of a machine, passed over a hot roller, and went on its way elsewhere. But he sat always in one place, beyond the reach

66

of daylight, a gas-jet flaring over him, himself part of the mechanism.

He was very happy at that job, in spite of the moist heat, for he was still young and in possession of dreams and illusions. And wonderful dreams he dreamed as he watched the streaming cloth streaming endlessly by. But there was no exercise about the work, no call upon his mind, and he dreamed less and less, while his mind grew torpid and drowsy. Nevertheless, he earned two dollars a week, and two dollars represented the difference between acute starvation and chronic underfeeding.

But when he was nine, he lost his job. Measles was the cause of it. After he recovered, he got work in a glass factory. The pay was better, and the work demanded skill. It was piecework, and the more skilful he was, the bigger wages he earned. Here was incentive. And under this incentive he developed into a remarkable worker.

It was simple work, the tying of glass stoppers into small bottles. At his waist he carried a bundle of twine. He held the bottle between his knees so that he might work with both hands. Thus, in a sitting position and bending over his own knees, his narrow shoulders grew humped and his chest was contracted for ten hours each day. This was not good for the lungs, but he tied three hundred dozen bottles a day.

The superintendent was very proud of him, and brought visitors to look at him. In ten hours three hundred dozen bottles passed through his hands. This meant that he had attained machine-like perfection. All waste movements were eliminated. Every motion of his thin arms, every movement of a muscle in the thin fingers, was swift and accurate. He worked at high tension, and the result was that he grew nervous. At night his muscles twitched in his sleep, and in the daytime he could not relax and rest. He remained keyed up and his muscles continued to twitch. Also he grew sallow and his lint-cough grew worse. Then pneumonia laid hold of the feeble lungs within the contracted chest, and he lost his job in the glass-works.

Now he had returned to the jute mills where he had first begun with winding bobbins. But promotion was waiting for him. He was a good worker. He would next go on the starcher, and later he would go into the loom room. There was nothing after that except increased efficiency.

The machinery ran faster than when he had first gone to work, and his mind ran slower. He no longer dreamed at all, though his earlier years had been full of dreaming. Once he had been in love. It was when he first began guiding the cloth over the hot roller, and it was with the daughter of the superintendent. She was much older than he, a young woman, and he had seen her at a distance only a paltry half-dozen times. But that made no difference. On the surface of the cloth stream that poured past him, he pictured radiant futures wherein he performed prodigies of toil, invented miraculous machines, won to the mastership of the mills, and in the end took her in his arms and kissed her soberly on the brow.

But that was all in the long ago, before he had grown too old and tired to love. Also, she had married and gone away, and his mind had gone to sleep. Yet it had been a wonderful experience and he used often to look back upon it as other men and women look back upon the time they believed in fairies. He had never believed in fairies nor Santa Claus; but he had believed implicitly in the smiling future his imagination had wrought into the streaming cloth stream.

He had become a man very early in life. At seven, when he drew his first wages, began his adolescence. A certain feeling of independence crept up in him, and the relationship between him and his mother changed. Somehow, as an earner and breadwinner, doing his own work in the world, he was more than an equal with her. Manhood, full-blown manhood, had come when he was eleven, at which time he had gone to work on the night shift for six months. No child works on the night shift and remains a child.

There had been several great events in his life. One of these had been when his mother bought some California prunes. Two others had been the two times when she cooked custard. Those had been events. He remembered them kindly. And at that same time his mother had told him of a blissful dish she would sometime make—'floating island', she had called it, 'better than custard'. For years he had looked forward to the day when he would sit down to the table with floating island before him, until, at last, he had relegated the idea of it to the limbo of unattainable ideals

Once he found a silver quarter lying on the sidewalk. That, also, was a great event in his life, withal a tragic one. He knew his duty on the instant the silver flashed on his eyes, before even he had picked it up. At home, as usual, there was not enough to eat, and home he should have taken it as he did his wages every Saturday night. Right conduct in this case was obvious; but he never had any spending of his money, and he was suffering from candy hunger. He was ravenous for the sweets that only on red-letter days he had ever tasted in his life.

He did not attempt to deceive himself. He knew it was a sin, and deliberately he sinned when he went on a fifteen-cent candy debauch. Ten cents he saved for a future orgy; but not being accustomed to the carrying of money, he lost the ten cents. This occurred at the time when he was suffering all the torments of conscience, and it was to him an act of divine retribution. He had a frightened sense of the closeness of an awful and wrathful God. God had seen, and God had been swift to punish, denying him even the full wages of sin.

In memory he always looked back upon that event as the one great criminal deed of his life, and at the recollection his conscience always awoke and gave him another twinge. It was the skeleton in his closet. Also, being so made and circumstanced, he looked back upon the deed with regret. He was dissatisfied with the manner in which he had spent the quarter. He could have invested it better, and, out of his later knowledge of the quickness of God, he would have beaten God out by spending the whole quarter at one fell swoop. In retrospect he spent the quarter a thousand times, and each time to better advantage.

There was another memory of the past, dim and faded, but stamped into his soul everlasting by the savage feet of his father. It was more like a nightmare than a remembered vision of a concrete thing—more like the race-memory of man that makes him fall in his sleep and that goes back to his arboreal ancestry.

This particular memory never came to Johnny in broad daylight when he was awake. It came at night, in bed, at the moment that his consciousness was sinking down and losing itself in sleep. It always aroused him to frightened wakefulness, and for the moment, in the first sickening start, it seemed to him that he lay crosswise on the foot of the bed. In the bed were the vague forms of his father and mother. He never saw what his father looked like. He had but one impression of his father, and that was that he had savage and pitiless feet.

His earlier memories lingered with him, but he had no late memories. All days were alike. Yesterday or last year were the same as a thousand years—or a minute. Nothing ever happened. There were no events to mark the march of time. Time did not march. It stood always still. It was only the whirling machines that moved, and they moved nowhere—in spite of the fact that they moved faster.

When he was fourteen, he went to work on the starcher. It

was a colossal event. Something had at last happened that could be remembered beyond a night's sleep or a week's pay-day. It marked an era. It was a machine Olympiad, a thing to date from. 'When I went to work on the starcher', or 'after', or 'before I went to work on the starcher', were sentences often on his lips.

He celebrated his sixteenth birthday by going into the loom room and taking a loom. Here was an incentive again, for it was piece-work. And he excelled, because the clay of him had been moulded by the mills into the perfect machine. At the end of three months he was running two looms, and, later, three and four.

At the end of his second year at the looms he was turning out more yards than any other weaver, and more than twice as much as some of the less skilful ones. And at home things began to prosper as he approached the full stature of his earning power. Not, however, that his increased earnings were in excess of need. The children were growing up. They ate more. And they were going to school, and school-books cost money. And somehow, the faster he worked, the faster climbed the price of things. Even the rent went up, though the house had fallen from bad to worse disrepair.

He had grown taller; but with his increased height he seemed leaner than ever. Also, he was more nervous. With the nervousness increased his peevishness and irritability. The children had learned by many bitter lessons to fight shy of him. His mother respected him for his earning power, but somehow her respect was tinctured with fear.

There was no joyousness in life for him. The procession of the days he never saw. The nights he slept away in twitching unconsciousness. The rest of the time he worked, and his consciousness was machine consciousness. Outside this his mind was a blank. He had no ideals, and but one illusion: namely, that he drank excellent coffee. He was a work-beast. He had no mental life whatever; yet deep down in the crypts of his mind, unknown to him, were being weighed and sifted every hour of his toil, every movement of his hands, every twitch of his muscles, and preparations were making for a future course of action that would amaze him and all his little world.

It was in the late spring that he came home from work one night aware of unusual tiredness. There was a keen expectancy in the air as he sat down to the table, but he did not notice. He went through the meal in moody silence, mechanically eating what was before him. The children um'd and ah'd and made smacking noises with their mouths. But he was deaf to them.

'D'ye know what you're eatin'?' his mother demanded at last, desperately.

He looked vacantly at the dish before him, and vacantly at her.

'Floatin' island,' she announced triumphantly.

'Oh,' he said.

'Floating island!' the children chorused loudly.

'Oh,' he said. And after two or three mouthfuls, he added, 'I guess I ain't hungry tonight.'

He dropped the spoon, shoved back his chair, and arose wearily from the table.

'An' I guess I'll go to bed.'

His feet dragged more heavily than usual as he crossed the kitchen floor. Undressing was a Titan's task, a monstrous futility, and he wept weakly as he crawled into bed, one shoe still on. He was aware of a rising, swelling something inside his head that made his brain thick and fuzzy. His lean fingers felt as big as his wrist, while in the ends of them was a remoteness of sensation vague and fuzzy like his brain. The small of his back ached intolerably. All his bones ached. He ached everywhere. And in his head began the shrieking, pounding, crashing, roaring of a million looms. All space was filled with flying shuttles. They darted in and out, intricately, amongst the stars. He worked a thousand looms himself, and ever they speeded up, faster and faster, and his brain unwound, faster and faster, and became the thread that fed the thousand flying shuttles.

He did not go to work next morning. He was too busy weaving colossally on the thousand looms that ran inside his head. His mother went to work, but first she sent for the doctor. It was a severe attack of la grippe, he said. Jennie served as nurse and carried out his instructions.

It was a very severe attack, and it was a week before Johnny dressed and tottered feebly across the floor. Another week, the doctor said, and he would be fit to return to work. The foreman of the loom room visited him on Sunday afternoon, the first day of his convalescence. The best weaver in the room, the foreman told his mother. His job would be held for him. He could come back to work a week from Monday.

'Why don't you thank 'im, Johnny?' his mother asked anxiously.

'He's ben that sick he ain't himself yet,' she explained apologetically to the visitor.

Johnny sat hunched up and gazing steadfastly at the floor. He sat in the same position long after the foreman had gone. It was warm outdoors, and he sat on the stoop in the afternoon. Sometimes his lips moved. He seemed lost in endless calculations.

Next morning, after the day grew warm, he took his seat on the stoop. He had pencil and paper this time with which to continue his calculations, and he calculated painfully and amazingly.

'What comes after millions?' he asked at noon, when Will came home from school. 'An' how d'ye work 'em?'

That afternoon finished his task. Each day, but without paper and pencil, he returned to the stoop. He was greatly absorbed in the one tree that grew across the street. He studied it for hours at a time, and was unusually interested when the wind swayed its branches and fluttered its leaves. Throughout the week he seemed lost in a great communion with himself. On Sunday, sitting on the stoop, he laughed aloud, several times, to the perturbation of his mother, who had not heard him laugh for years.

Next morning, in the early darkness, she came to his bed to rouse him. He had had his fill of sleep all the week, and awoke easily. He made no struggle, nor did he attempt to hold on to the bedding when she stripped it from him. He lay quietly, and spoke quietly.

'It ain't no use, ma.'

'You'll be late,' she said, under the impression that he was still stupid with sleep.

'I'm awake, ma, an' I tell you it ain't no use. You might as well lemme alone. I ain't goin' to git up.'

'But you'll lose your job!' she cried.

'I ain't goin' to git up,' he repeated in a strange, passionless voice.

She did not go to work herself that morning. This was sickness beyond any sickness she had ever known. Fever and delirium she could understand; but this was insanity. She pulled the bedding up over him and sent Jennie for the doctor.

When that person arrived, Johnny was sleeping gently, and gently he awoke and allowed his pulse to be taken.

'Nothing the matter with him,' the doctor reported. 'Badly debilitated, that's all. Not much meat on his bones.'

'He's always been that way,' his mother volunteered.

'Now go 'way, ma, an' let me finish my snooze.'

Johnny spoke sweetly and placidly, and sweetly and placidly he rolled over on his side and went to sleep.

At ten o'clock he awoke and dressed himself. He walked out into the kitchen, where he found his mother with a frightened expression on her face.

'I'm goin' away, ma,' he announced, 'an' I jes' want to say goodbye.'

She threw her apron over her head and sat down suddenly and wept. He waited patiently.

'I might a-known it,' she was sobbing.

'Where?' she finally asked, removing the apron from her head and gazing up at him with a stricken face in which there was little curiosity.

'I don't know—anywhere.'

As he spoke, the tree across the street appeared with dazzling brightness on his inner vision. It seemed to lurk just under his eyelids and he could see it whenever he wished.

'An' your job?' she quavered.

'I ain't never goin' to work again.'

'My God, Johnny!' she wailed, 'don't say that!'

What he had said was blasphemy to her. As a mother who hears her child deny God, was Johnny's mother shocked by his words.

'What's got into you, anyway?' she demanded, with a lame attempt at imperativeness.

'Figures,' he answered. 'Jes' figures. I've ben doin' a lot of figurin' this week, an' it's most surprisin'.'

'I don't see what that's got to do with it,' she sniffled.

Johnny smiled patiently, and his mother was aware of a distinct shock at the persistent absence of his peevishness and irritability.

'I'll show you,' he said. 'I'm plum' tired out. What makes me tired? Moves. I've ben movin' ever since I was born. I'm tired of movin', an' I ain't goin' to move any more. Remember when I worked in the glass-house? I used to do three hundred dozen a day. Now I reckon I made about ten different moves to each bottle. That's thirty-six thousan' moves a day. Ten days three hundred an' sixty thousan' moves. One month, one million an' eighty thousan' moves. Chuck out the eighty thousan''—he spoke with the complacent beneficence of a philanthropist—'chuck out the eighty thousan', that leaves a million moves in a month—twelve million moves a year.

'At the looms I'm movin' twic'st as much. That makes

twenty-five million moves a year, an' it seems to me I've ben a movin' that way 'most a million years.

'Now this week I ain't moved at all. I ain't made one move in hours an' hours. I tell you it was swell, jes' settin' there, hours an' hours, an' doin' nothin'. I ain't never ben happy before. I never had any time. I've ben movin' all the time. That ain't no way to be happy. An' I ain't going to do it any more. I'm jes' goin' to set, an' set, an' rest, an' rest, and then rest some more.'

'But what's goin' to come of Will an' the children?' she asked despairingly.

'That's it, "Will an' the children," ' he repeated. But there was no bitterness in his voice. He had long known his mother's ambition for the younger boy, but the thought of it no longer rankled. Nothing mattered any more. Not even that.

'I know, ma, what you've ben plannin' for Will—keepin' him to school to make a book-keeper out of him. But it ain't no use, I've quit. He's got to go to work.'

'An' after I have brung you up the way I have,' she wept, starting to cover her head with the apron and changing her mind.

'You never brung me up,' he answered with sad kindliness. 'I brung myself up, ma, an' I brung up Will. He's bigger'n me, an' heavier, an' taller. When I was a kid, I reckon I didn't git enough to eat. When he come along an' was a kid, I was workin' an' earnin' grub for him too. But that's done with. Will can go to work, same as me, or he can go to hell. I don't care which. I'm tired. I'm going now. Ain't you goin' to say goodbye?'

She made no reply. The apron had gone over her head again, and she was crying. He paused a moment in the doorway.

'I'm sure I done the best I knew how,' she was sobbing.

He passed out of the house and down the street. A wan delight came into his face at the sight of the lone tree. 'Jes' ain't goin' to do nothin',' he said to himself, half aloud, in a crooning tone. He glanced wistfully up at the sky, but the bright sun dazzled and blinded him.

It was a long walk he took, and he did not walk fast. It took him past the jute-mill. The muffled roar of the loom-room came to his ears and he smiled. It was a gentle, placid smile. He hated no one, not even the pounding, shrieking machines. There was no bitterness in him, nothing but an inordinate hunger for rest.

The houses and factories thinned out and the open spaces increased as he approached the country. At last the city was behind him, and he was walking down a leafy lane beside the railroad track. He did not walk like a man. He did not look like a man. He was a travesty of the human. It was a twisted and stunted and nameless piece of life that shambled like a sickly ape, arms loose-hanging, stoop-shouldered, narrow-chested, grotesque and terrible.

He passed by a small railroad station and lay down in the grass under a tree. All afternoon he lay there. Sometimes he dozed, with muscles that twitched in his sleep. When awake, he lay without movement, watching the birds or looking up at the sky through the branches of the tree above him. Once or twice he laughed aloud, but without relevance to anything he had seen or felt.

After twilight had gone in the first darkness of the night, a freight train rumbled into the station. When the engine was switching cars on to the side-track, Johnny crept along the side of the train. He pulled open the side-door of an empty box-car and awkwardly and laboriously climbed in. He closed the door. The engine whistled. Johnny was lying down, and in the darkness he smiled.

Semper Idem

Doctor Bicknell was in a remarkably gracious mood. Through a minor accident, a slight bit of carelessness, that was all, a man who might have pulled through had died the preceding night. Though it had been only a sailorman, one of the innumerable unwashed, the steward of the receiving hospital had been on the anxious seat all the morning. It was not that the man had died that gave him discomfort, he knew the doctor too well for that, but his distress lay in the fact that the operation had been done so well. One of the most delicate in surgery, it had been as successful as it was clever and audacious. All had then depended upon the treatment, the nurses, the steward. And the man had died. Nothing much, a bit of carelessness, yet enough to bring the professional wrath of Doctor Bicknell about his ears and to perturb the working of the staff and nurses for twenty-four hours to come.

But, as already stated, the Doctor was in a remarkably gracious mood. When informed by the steward, in fear and trembling, of the man's unexpected take-off, his lips did not so much as form one syllable of censure; nay, they were so pursed that snatches of rag-time floated softly from them, to be broken only by a pleasant query after the health of the other's eldest-born. The steward, deeming it impossible that he could have caught the gist of the case, repeated it.

77

'Yes, yes,' Doctor Bicknell said impatiently; 'I understand. But how about Semper Idem? Is he ready to leave?'

'Yes. They're helping him to dress now,' the steward answered, passing on to the round of his duties, content that peace still reigned within the iodine-saturated walls.

It was Semper Idem's recovery which had so fully compensated Doctor Bicknell for the loss of the sailorman. Lives were to him as nothing, the unpleasant but inevitable incidents of the profession, but cases, ah, cases were everything. People who knew him were prone to brand him a butcher, but his colleagues were at one in the belief that a bolder and yet a more capable man never stood over the table. He was not an imaginative man. He did not possess, and hence had no tolerance for emotion. His nature was accurate, precise, scientific. Men were to him no more than pawns, without individuality or personal value. But as cases it was different. The more broken a man was, the more precarious his grip on life, the greater his significance in the eyes of Doctor Bicknell. He would as readily forsake a poet laureate suffering from a common accident for a nameless, mangled vagrant who defied every law of life by refusing to die as would a child forsake a Punch and Judy for a circus.

So it had been in the case of Semper Idem. The mystery of the man had not appealed to him, nor had his silence and the veiled romance which the yellow reporters had so sensationally and so fruitlessly exploited in divers Sunday editions. But Semper Idem's throat had been cut. That was the point. That was where his interest had centred. Cut from ear to ear, and not one surgeon in a thousand to give a snap of the fingers for his chance of recovery. But, thanks to the swift municipal ambulance service and to Doctor Bicknell, he had been dragged back into the world he had sought to leave. The Doctor's co-workers had shaken their heads when the case was brought in. Impossible, they said. Throat, wind-pipe, jugular all but actually severed and the loss of blood frightful. As it was such a foregone conclusion, Doctor Bicknell had employed methods and done things which made them, even in their professional capacities, to shudder. And lo, the man had recovered.

So, on this morning that Semper Idem was to leave the hospital, hale and hearty, Doctor Bicknell's geniality was in nowise disturbed by the steward's report, and he proceeded cheerfully to bring order out of the chaos of a child's body which had been ground and crunched beneath the wheels of an electric car.

SEMPER IDEM

As many will remember, the case of Semper Idem aroused a vast deal of unseemly yet highly natural curiosity. He had been found in a slum lodging, with throat cut as aforementioned, and blood dripping down upon the inmates of the room below and disturbing their festivities. He had evidently done the deed standing, with head bowed forward that he might gaze his last upon a photograph which stood on the table propped against a candlestick. It was this attitude which had made it possible for Doctor Bicknell to save him. So terrific had been the sweep of the razor that had he had his head thrown back, as he should have done to have accomplished the act properly, with his neck stretched and the elastic vascular walls distended, he would have of a certainty well nigh decapitated himself.

At the hospital, during all the time he travelled the repugnant road back to life, not a word had left his lips. Nor could anything be learned of him by the sleuths detailed by the chief of police. Nobody knew him, nor had ever seen or heard of him before. He was strictly, uniquely, of the present. His clothes and surroundings were those of the lowest labourer, his hands the hands of a gentleman. But not a shred of writing was discovered, nothing, save in one particular, which would serve to indicate his past or his position in life.

And that one particular was the photograph. If it were at all a likeness, the woman who gazed frankly out upon the on-looker from the card-mount must have been a striking creature indeed. It was an amateur production, for the detectives were baffled in that no professional photographer's signature or studio was appended. Across a corner of the mount, in delicate feminine tracery, was written: '*Semper idem; semper fidelis.*' And she looked it. As many recollect, it was a face one could never forget. Clever half-tones, remarkably like, were published in all the leading papers at the time; but such procedure gave rise to nothing but the uncontrollable public curiosity and interminable copy to the space-writers.

For want of a better name, the rescued suicide was known to the hospital attendants and to the world as Semper Idem. And Semper Idem he remained. Reporters, detectives and nurses gave him up in despair. Not one word could he be persuaded to utter; yet the flitting conscious light of his eyes showed that his ears heard and his brain grasped every question put to him.

But this mystery and romance played no part in Doctor Bicknell's interest when he paused in the office to have a parting word with his patient. He, the Doctor, had performed a prodigy in the matter of this man, done what was virtually unprecedented in the annals of surgery. He did not care who or what the man was, and it was highly improbable that he should ever see him again; but, like the artist gazing upon a finished creation, he wished to look for the last time upon the work of his hand and brain.

Semper Idem still remained mute. He seemed anxious to be gone. Not a word could the Doctor extract from him, and little the Doctor cared. He examined the throat of the convalescent carefully, idling over the hideous scar with the lingering, half-caressing fondness of a parent. It was not a particularly pleasing sight. An angry line circled the throat—for all the world as though the man had just escaped the hangman's noose—and, disappearing below the ear on either side, had the appearance of completing the fiery periphery at the nape of the neck.

Maintaining his dogged silence, yielding to the other's examination in much the manner of a leashed lion, Semper Idem betrayed only his desire to drop from out of the public eye.

"Well, I'll not keep you,' Doctor Bicknell finally said, laying a hand on the man's shoulder and stealing a last glance at his own handiwork. 'But let me give you a bit of advice. Next time you try it on, hold your chin up, so. Don't snuggle it down and butcher yourself like a cow. Neatness and despatch you know. Neatness and despatch.'

Semper Idem's eyes flashed in token that he had heard and a moment later the hospital door swung to on his heel.

It was a busy day for Doctor Bicknell and the afternoon was well along when he lighted a cigar preparatory to leaving the table upon which it seemed the sufferers almost clamoured to be laid. But the last one, an old rag-picker with a broken shoulder-blade, had been disposed of, and the first fragrant smoke wreaths had begun to curl about his head when the gong of a hurrying ambulance came through the open window from the street, followed by the inevitable entry of the stretcher with its ghastly freight.

'Lay it on the table,' the Doctor directed, turning for a moment to place his cigar in safety. 'What is it?'

'Suicide—cut throat,' responded one of the stretcher bearers. 'Down on Morgan Alley. Little hope, I think, sir. He's 'most gone.'

'Eh? Well, I'll give him a look, anyway.' He leaned over the man at the moment when the quick made its last faint flutter and succumbed.

'It's Semper Idem come back again,' the steward said.

'Ay,' replied Doctor Bicknell, 'and gone again. No bungling this time. Properly done, upon my life, sir, properly done. Took my advice to the letter. I'm not required here. Take it along to the morgue.'

Doctor Bicknell secured his cigar and relighted it. 'That,' he said between the puffs, looking at the steward, 'that evens up for the one you lost last night. We're quits now.'

Told in the Drooling Ward

Me? I'm not a drooler. I'm the assistant. I don't know what Miss Jones or Miss Kelsey could do without me. There are fifty-five low-grade droolers in this ward, and how could they ever all be fed if I wasn't around? I like to feed droolers. They don't make trouble. They can't. Something's wrong with most of their legs and arms, and they can't talk. They're very low-grade. I can walk, and talk, and do things. You must be careful with the droolers and not feed them too fast. Then they choke. Miss Jones says I'm an expert. When a new nurse comes I show her how to do it. It's funny watching a new nurse try to feed them. She goes at it so slow and careful that supper time would be around before she finished shoving down their breakfast. Then I show her, because I'm an expert. Dr. Dalrymple says I am, and he ought to know. A drooler can eat twice as fast if you know how to make him.

My name's Tom. I'm twenty-eight years old. Everybody knows me in the institution. This is an institution, you know. It belongs to the State of California and is run by politics. I know. I've been here a long time. Everybody trusts me. I run errands all over the place, when I'm not busy with the droolers. I like droolers. It makes me think how lucky I am that I ain't a drooler.

I like it here in the Home. I don't like the outside. I know. I've been around a bit, and run away, and adopted. Me for the

Home, and for the drooling ward best of all. I don't look like a drooler, do I? You can tell the difference soon as you look at me. I'm an assistant, expert assistant. That's going some for a feeb. Feeb? Oh, that's feeble-minded. I thought you knew. We're all feebs in here.

But I'm a high-grade feeb. Dr. Dalrymple says I'm too smart to be in the Home, but I never let on. It's a pretty good place. And I don't throw fits like lots of the feebs. You see that house up there through the trees. The high-grade epilecs all live in it by themselves. They're stuck up because they ain't ordinary feebs. They call it the club house, and they say they're just as good as anybody outside, only they're sick. I don't like them much. They laugh at me, when they ain't busy throwing fits. But I don't care. I never have to be scared about falling down and busting my head. Sometimes they run around in circles trying to find a place to sit down quick, only they don't. Low-grade epilecs are disgusting, and high-grade epilecs put on airs. I'm glad I ain't an epilec. There ain't anything to them. They just talk big, that's all.

Miss Kelsey says I talk too much. But I talk sense, and that's more than the other feebs do. Dr. Dalrymple says I have the gift of language. I know it. You ought to hear me talk when I'm by myself, or when I've got a drooler to listen. Sometimes I think I'd like to be a politician, only it's too much trouble. They're all great talkers; that's how they hold their jobs.

Nobody's crazy in this institution. They're just feeble in their minds. Let me tell you something funny. There's about a dozen high-grade girls that set the tables in the big dining-room. Sometimes when they're done ahead of time, they all sit down in chairs in a circle and talk. I sneak up to the door and listen, and I nearly die to keep from laughing. Do you want to know what they talk? It's like this. They don't say a word for a long time. And then one says, 'Thank God I'm not feeble-minded.' And all the rest nod their heads and look pleased. And then nobody says anything for a time. After which the next girl in the circle says, 'Thank God I'm not feeble-minded,' and they nod their heads all over again. And it goes on around the circle, and they never say anything else. Now they're real feebs, ain't they? I leave it to you. I'm not that kind of a feeb, thank God.

Sometimes I don't think I'm a feeb at all. I play in the band and read music. We're all supposed to be feebs in the band except the leader. He's crazy. We know it, but we never talk about it except amongst ourselves. His job is politics, too, and we don't want him to lose it. I play the drum. They can't get along without me in this institution. I was sick once, so I know. It's a wonder the drooling ward didn't break down while I was in hospital.

I could get out of here if I wanted to. I'm not so feeble as some might think. But I don't let on. I have too good a time. Besides, everything would run down if I went away. I'm afraid some time they'll find out I'm not a feeb and send me out into the world to earn my own living. I know the world, and I don't like it. The Home is fine enough for me.

You see how I grin sometimes. I can't help that. But I can put it on a lot. I'm not bad, though. I look at myself in the glass. My mouth is funny, I know that, and it lops down, and my teeth are bad. You can tell a feeb anywhere by looking at his mouth and teeth. But that doesn't prove I'm a feeb. It's just because I'm lucky that I look like one.

I know a lot. If I told you all I know, you'd be surprised. But when I don't want to know, or when they want me to do something I don't want to do, I just let my mouth lop down and laugh and make foolish noises. I watch the foolish noises made by the low-grades, and I can fool anybody. And I know a lot of foolish noises. Miss Kelsey called me a fool the other day. She was very angry, and that was where I fooled her.

Miss Kelsey asked me once why I don't write a book about feebs. I was telling her what was the matter with little Albert. He's a drooler, you know, and I can always tell the way he twists his left eye what's the matter with him. So I was explaining it to Miss Kelsey, and, because she didn't know, it made her mad. But some day, mebbe, I'll write that book. Only it's so much trouble. Besides, I'd sooner talk.

Do you know what a micro is? It's the kind with the little heads no bigger than your fist. They're usually droolers, and they live a long time. The hydros don't drool. They have the big heads, and they're smarter. But they never grow up. They always die. I never look at one without thinking he's going to die. Sometimes, when I'm feeling lazy, or the nurse is mad at me, I wish I was a drooler with nothing to do and somebody to feed me. But I guess I'd sooner talk and be what I am.

Only yesterday Dr. Dalrymple said to me, 'Tom,' he said, 'I just don't know what I'd do without you.' And he ought to know, seeing as he's had the bossing of a thousand feebs for going on two years. Dr. Whatcomb was before him. They get appointed, you know. It's politics. I've seen a whole lot of doctors here in my time. I was here before any of them. I've been in this institution twenty-five years. No, I've got no complaints. The institution couldn't be run better.

It's a snap to be a high-grade feeb. Just look at Dr. Dalrymple. He has troubles. He holds his job by politics. You bet we high-graders talk politics. We know all about it, and it's bad. An institution like this oughtn't to be run on politics. Look at Dr. Dalrymple. He's been here two years and learned a lot. Then politics will come along and throw him out and send a new doctor who don't know anything about feebs.

I've been acquainted with just thousands of nurses in my time. Some of them are nice. But they come and go. Most of the women get married. Sometimes I think I'd like to get married. I spoke to Dr. Whatcomb about it once, but he told me he was very sorry, because feebs ain't allowed to get married. I've been in love. She was a nurse. I won't tell you her name. She had blue eyes, and yellow hair, and a kind voice, and she liked me. She told me so. And she always told me to be a good boy. And I was, too, until afterwards, and then I ran away. You see, she went off and got married, and she didn't tell me about it.

I guess being married ain't what it's cracked up to be. Dr. Anglin and his wife used to fight. I've seen them. And once I heard her call him a feeb. Now nobody has a right to call anybody a feeb that ain't. Dr. Anglin got awful mad when she called him that. But he didn't last long. Politics drove him out, and Dr. Mandeville came. He didn't have a wife. I heard him talking one time with the engineer. The engineer and his wife fought like cats and dogs, and that day Dr. Mandeville told him he was damn glad he wasn't tied to no petticoats. A petticoat is a skirt. I knew what he meant, if I was a feeb. But I never let on. You hear lots when you don't let on.

I've seen a lot in my time. Once I was adopted, and went away on the railroad over forty miles to live with a man named Peter Bopp and his wife. They had a ranch. Dr. Anglin said I was strong and bright, and I said I was, too. That was because I wanted to be adopted. And Peter Bopp said he'd give me a good home, and the lawyers fixed up the papers.

But I soon made up my mind that a ranch was no place for me. Mrs. Bopp was scared to death of me and wouldn't let me sleep in the house. They fixed up the woodshed and made me sleep there. I had to get up at four o'clock and feed the horses, and milk cows, and carry the milk to the neighbours. They called it chores, but it kept me going all day. I chopped wood, and cleaned chicken houses, and weeded vegetables, and did most everything on the place. I never had any fun. I hadn't no time.

Let me tell you one thing. I'd sooner feed mush and milk to feebs than milk cows with the frost on the ground. Mrs. Bopp was scared to let me play with her children. And I was scared, too. They used to make faces at me when nobody was looking, and call me 'Looney'. Everybody called me Looney Tom. And the other boys in the neighbourhood threw rocks at me. You never see anything like that in the Home here. The feebs are better behaved.

Mrs. Bopp used to pinch me and pull my hair when she thought I was too slow, and I only made foolish noises and went slower. She said I'd be the death of her some day. I left the boards off the old well in the pasture, and the pretty new calf fell in and got drowned. Then Peter Bopp said he was going to give me a licking. He did, too. He took a strap halter and went at me. It was awful. I'd never had a licking in my life. They don't do such things in the Home, which is why I say the Home is the place for me.

I know the law, and I knew he had no right to lick me with a strap halter. That was being cruel, and the guardianship papers said he mustn't be cruel. I didn't say anything. I just waited, which shows you what kind of a feeb I am. I waited a long time, and got slower, and made more foolish noises; but he wouldn't send me back to the Home, which was what I wanted. But one day, it was the first of the month, Mrs. Brown gave me three dollars, which was for her milk bill with Peter Bopp. That was in the morning. When I brought the milk in the evening I was to bring back the receipt. But I didn't. I just walked down to the station, bought a ticket like anyone, and rode on the train back to the Home. That's the kind of feeb I am.

Dr. Anglin was gone then, and Dr. Mandeville had his place. I walked right into his office. He didn't know me. 'Hello,' he said, 'this ain't visiting day.' 'I ain't no visitor,' I said. 'I'm Tom. I belong here.' Then he whistled and showed he was surprised. I told him all about it, and showed him the marks of the strap halter, and he got madder and madder all the time and said he'd attend to Mr. Peter Bopp's case.

And mebbe you think some of them little droolers weren't glad to see me.

I walked right into the ward. There was a new nurse feeding little Albert. 'Hold on,' I said. 'That ain't the way. Don't you see how he's twisting that left eye? Let me show you.' Mebbe she thought I was a new doctor, for she just gave me the spoon, and I guess I filled little Albert up with the most comfortable meal he'd had since I went away. Droolers ain't bad when you understand them. I heard Miss Jones tell Miss Kelsey once that I had an amazing gift in handling droolers.

Some day, mebbe, I'm going to talk with Dr. Dalrymple and get him to give me a declaration that I ain't a feeb. Then I'll get him to make me a real assistant in the drooling ward, with forty dollars a month and my board. And then I'll marry Miss Jones and live right here. And if she won't have me, I'll marry Miss Kelsey or some other nurse. There's lots of them that want to get married. And I won't care if my wife gets mad and calls me a feeb. What's the good? And I guess when one's learned to put up with droolers a wife won't be much worse.

I didn't tell you about when I ran away. I hadn't no idea of such a thing, and it was Charley and Joe who put me up to it. They're high-grade epilecs, you know. I'd been up to Dr. Wilson's office with a message, and was going back to the drooling ward, when I saw Charley and Joe hiding around the corner of the gymnasium and making motions to me. I went over to them.

'Hello,' Joe said. 'How's droolers?'

'Fine,' I said. 'Had any fits lately?'

That made them mad, and I was going on, when Joe said, 'We're running away. Come on.'

'What for?' I said.

'We're going up over the top of the mountain,' Joe said.

'And find a gold mine,' said Charley. 'We don't have fits any more. We're cured.'

'All right,' I said. And we sneaked around back of the gymnasium and in among the trees. Mebbe we walked along about ten minutes, when I stopped.

'What's the matter?' said Joe.

'Wait,' I said. 'I got to go back.'

'What for? said Joe.

And I said, 'To get little Albert.'

And they said I couldn't, and got mad. But I didn't care. I knew they'd wait. You see, I've been here twenty-five years, and I know the back trails that lead up the mountain, and Charley and Joe didn't know those trails. That's why they wanted me to come.

So I went back and got little Albert. He can't walk, or talk, or do anything except drool, and I had to carry him in my arms. We went on past the last hayfield which was as far as

I'd ever gone. Then the woods and brush got so thick, and me not finding any more trail, we followed the cow-path down to a big creek and crawled through the fence which showed where the Home land stopped.

We climbed up the big hill on the other side of the creek. It was all big trees, and no brush, but it was so steep and slippery with dead leaves we could hardly walk. By and by we came to a real bad place. It was forty feet across, and if you slipped you'd fall a thousand feet, or mebbe a hundred. Anyway, you wouldn't fall—just slide. I went across first, carrying little Albert. Joe came next. But Charley got scared right in the middle and sat down.

'I'm going to have a fit,' he said.

'No, you're not,' said Joe. 'Because if you was you wouldn't 'a' sat down. You take all your fits standin.'

'This is a different kind of a fit,' said Charley, beginning to cry.

He shook and shook, but just because he wanted to he couldn't scare up the least kind of a fit.

Joe got mad and used awful language. But that didn't help none. So I talked soft and kind to Charley. That's the way to handle feebs. If you get mad, they get worse. I know. I'm that way myself. That's why I was almost the death of Mrs. Bopp. She got mad.

It was getting along in the afternoon, and I knew we had to be on our way, so I said to Joe:

'Here, stop your cussing and hold Albert. I'll go back and get him.'

And I did, too; but he was so scared and dizzy he crawled along on hands and knees while I helped him. When I got him across and took Albert back in my arms, I heard somebody laugh and looked down. And there was a man and woman on horseback looking up at us. He had a gun on his saddle, and it was her who was laughing.

'Who in hell's that?' said Joe, getting scared. 'Somebody to catch us?'

'Shut up your cussing,' I said to him. 'That is the man who owns this ranch and writes books.'

'How do you do, Mr. Endicott?' I said down to him.

'Hello,' he said. 'What are you doing here?'

'We're running away.' I said.

And he said, 'Good luck. But be sure and get back before dark.'

'But this is a real running away,' I said.

And then both he and his wife laughed.

'All right,' he said. 'Good luck just the same. But watch out the bears and mountain lions don't get you when it gets dark.'

Then they rode away laughing, pleasant like; but I wished he hadn't said that about the bears and mountain lions.

After we got around the hill, I found a trail, and we went much faster. Charley didn't have any more signs of fits, and began laughing and talking about gold-mines. The trouble was with little Albert. He was almost as big as me. You see, all the time I'd been calling him little Albert, he'd been growing up. He was so heavy I couldn't keep up with Joe and Charley. I was all out of breath. So I told them they'd have to take turns in carrying him, which they said they wouldn't. Then I said I'd leave them and they'd get lost, and the mountain lions and bears would eat them. Charley looked like he was going to have a fit right there, and Joe said, 'Give him to me.' And after that we carried him in turn.

We kept right on up that mountain. I don't think there was any gold-mine, but we might 'a' got to the top and found it, if we hadn't lost the trail, and if it hadn't got dark, and if little Albert hadn't tired us all out carrying him. Lots of feebs are scared of the dark, and Joe said he was going to have a fit right there. Only he didn't. I never saw such an unlucky boy. He could never throw a fit when he wanted to. Some of the feebs can throw fits as quick as a wink.

By and by it got real black, and we were hungry, and we didn't have no fire. You see, they don't let feebs carry matches, and all we could do was just shiver. And we'd never thought about being hungry. You see, feebs always have their food ready for them, and that's why it's better to be a feeb than earning your living in the world.

And worse than everything was the quiet. There was only one thing worse, and it was the noises. There was all kinds of noises every once in a while, with quiet spells in between. I reckon they were rabbits, but they made noises in the brush like wild animals—you know, rustle rustle, thump, bump, crackle crackle, just like that. First Charley got a fit, a real one, and Joe threw a terrible one. I don't mind fits in the Home with everybody around. But out in the woods on a dark night is different. You listen to me, and never go hunting gold-mines with epilecs, even if they are high-grade.

I never had such an awful night. When Joe and Charley weren't throwing fits they were making believe, and in the darkness the shivers from the cold which I couldn't see seemed like fits, too. And I shivered so hard I thought I was getting fits myself. And little Albert, with nothing to eat, just drooled and drooled. I never seen him as bad as that before. Why, he twisted that left eye of his until it ought to have dropped out. I couldn't see it, but I could tell from the movements he made. And Joe just lay and cussed and cussed, and Charley cried and wished he was back in the Home.

We didn't die, and next morning we went right back the way we'd come. And little Albert got awful heavy. Dr. Wilson was mad as could be, and said I was the worst feeb in the institution, along with Joe and Charley. But Miss Striker, who was a nurse in the drooling ward then, just put her arms around me and cried, she was that happy I'd got back. I thought right there that mebbe I'd marry her. But only a month afterwards she got married to the plumber that came up from the city to fix the gutterpipes of the new hospital. And little Albert never twisted his eye for two days, it was that tired.

Next time I run away I'm going right over that mountain. But I ain't going to take epilecs along. They ain't never cured, and when they get scared or excited they throw fits to beat the band. But I'll take little Albert. Somehow I can't get along without him. And anyway, I ain't going to run away. The drooling ward's a better snap than gold-mines, and I hear there's a new nurse coming. Besides, little Albert's bigger than I am now, and I could never carry him over a mountain. And he's growing bigger every day. It's astonishing.

Make Westing

'Whatever you do, make westing! make westing!'
—*Sailing directions for Cape Horn*

For seven weeks the *Mary Rogers* had been between 50°
south in the Atlantic and 50° south in the Pacific, which
meant that for seven weeks she had been struggling to round
Cape Horn. For seven weeks she had been either in dirt, or
close to dirt, save once, and then, following upon six days of
excessive dirt, which she had ridden out under the shelter of
the redoubtable Terra del Fuego coast, she had almost gone
ashore during a heavy swell in the dead calm that had suddenly
fallen. For seven weeks she had wrestled with the Cape Horn
greybeards, and in return been buffeted and smashed by them.
She was a wooden ship, and her ceaseless straining had opened
her seams, so that twice a day the watch took its turn at the
pumps.

The *Mary Rogers* was strained, the crew was strained, and
big Dan Cullen, master, was likewise strained. Perhaps he was
strained most of all, for upon him rested the responsibility of
that titanic struggle. He slept most of the time in his clothes,
though he rarely slept. He haunted the deck at night, a great,
burly, robust ghost, black with the sunburn of thirty years of
sea and hairy as an orang-outang. He, in turn, was haunted by
one thought of action, a sailing direction for the Horn:
Whatever you do, make westing! make westing! It was an
obsession. He thought of nothing else, except, at times, to
blaspheme God for sending such bitter weather.

Make westing! He hugged the Horn, and a dozen times lay hove to with the iron Cape bearing east-by-north, or north-north-east, a score of miles away. And each time the eternal west wind smote him back and he made easting. He fought gale after gale, south to 64°, inside the antarctic drift-ice, and pledged his immortal soul to the Powers of Darkness, for a bit of westing, for a slant to take him around. And he made easting. In despair, he had tried to make the passage through the Straits of Le Maire. Halfway through, the wind hauled to the north'ard of north-west, the glass dropped to 28.88, and he turned and ran before a gale of cyclonic fury, missing, by a hair's breadth, piling up the *Mary Rogers* on the black-toothed rocks. Twice he had made west to the Diego Ramirez Rocks, one of the times saved between two snow-squalls by sighting the gravestones of ships a quarter of a mile dead ahead.

Blow! Captain Dan Cullen instanced all his thirty years at sea to prove that never had it blown so before. The *Mary Rogers* was hove to at the time he gave the evidence, and, to clinch it, inside half an hour the *Mary Rogers* was hove down to the hatches. Her new maintopsail and brand new spencer were blown away like tissue paper; and five sails, furled and fast under double gaskets, were blown loose and stripped from the yards. And, before morning the *Mary Rogers* was hove down twice again, and holes were knocked in her bulwarks to ease her decks from the weight of ocean that pressed her down.

On an average of once a week Captain Dan Cullen caught glimpses of the sun. Once, for ten minutes, the sun shone at midday, and ten minutes afterwards a new gale was piping up, both watches were shortening sail, and all was buried in the obscurity of a driving snow-squall. For a fortnight, once, Captain Dan Cullen was without a meridian or a chronometer sight. Rarely did he know his position within half of a degree, except when in sight of land; for sun and stars remained hidden behind the sky, and it was so gloomy that even at the best the horizons were poor for accurate observations. A grey gloom shrouded the world. The clouds were grey; the great driving seas were leaden grey; the smoking crests were a grey churning; even the occasional albatrosses were grey, while the snow-flurries were not white, but grey, under the sombre pall of the heavens.

Life on board the *Mary Rogers* was grey—grey and gloomy. The faces of the sailors were blue-grey; they were afflicted with sea-cats and sea-boils, and suffered exquisitely. They were shadows of men. For seven weeks, in the forecastle or on

93

deck, they had not known what it was to be dry. They had forgotten what it was to sleep out a watch, and all watches it was, 'All hands on deck!' They caught the snatches of agonized sleep, and they slept in their oil-skins ready for the everlasting call. So weak and worn were they that it took both watches to do the work of one. That was why both watches were on deck so much of the time. And no shadow of a man could shirk duty. Nothing less than a broken leg could enable a man to knock off work; and there were two such, who had been mauled and pulped by the seas that broke aboard.

One other man who was the shadow of a man was George Dorety. He was the only passenger on board, a friend of the firm, and he had elected to make the voyage for his health. But seven weeks off Cape Horn had not bettered his health. He gasped and panted in his bunk through the long, heaving nights; and when on deck he was so bundled up for warmth that he resembled a peripatetic old-clothes shop. At midday, eating at the cabin table in a gloom so deep that the swinging sea-lamps burned always, he looked as blue-grey as the sickest, saddest man for'ard. Nor did gazing across the table at Captain Dan Cullen have any cheering effect upon him. Captain Cullen chewed and scowled and kept silent. The scowls were for God, and with every chew he reiterated the sole thought of his existence, which was *make westing*. He was a big, hairy brute, and the sight of him was not stimulating to the other's appetite. He looked upon George Dorety as a Jonah, and told him so once each meal savagely transferring the scowl from God to the passenger and back again.

Nor did the mate prove a first aid to a languid appetite. Joshua Higgins by name, a seaman by profession and pull, but a pot-walloper by capacity, he was a loose-jointed, sniffling creature, heartless and selfish and cowardly, without a soul, in fear of his life of Dan Cullen, and a bully over the sailors, who knew that behind the mate was Captain Cullen, the law-giver and compeller, the driver and the destroyer, the incarnation of a dozen bucko mates. In that wild weather at the southern end of the earth, Joshua Higgins ceased washing. His grimy face usually robbed George Dorety of what little appetite he managed to accumulate. Ordinarily this lavatorial dereliction would have caught Captain Cullen's eye and vocabulary, but in the present his mind was filled with making westing, to the exclusion of all other things not contributory thereto. Whether the mate's face was clean or dirty had no bearing upon westing. Later on, when 50° south in the Pacific had been reached,

Joshua Higgins would wash his face very abruptly. In the meantime, at the cabin table, where grey twilight alternated with lamplight while the lamps were being filled, George Dorety sat between the two men, one a tiger and the other a hyena, and wondered why God had made them. The second mate, Matthew Turner, was a true sailor and a man, but George Dorety did not have the solace of his company, for he ate by himself, solitary, when they had finished.

On Saturday morning, July 24, George Dorety awoke to a feeling of life and headlong movement. On deck he found the *Mary Rogers* running off before a howling south-easter. Nothing was set but the lower topsails and the foresail. It was all she could stand, yet she was making fourteen knots, as Mr. Turner shouted in Dorety's ear when he came on deck. And it was all westing. She was going round the Horn at last ... if the wind held. Mr. Turner looked happy. The end of the struggle was in sight. But Captain Cullen did not look happy. He scowled at Dorety in passing. Captain Cullen did not want God to know that he was pleased with that wind. He had a conception of a malicious God, and believed in his secret soul that if God knew it was a desirable wind, God would promptly efface it and send a snorter from the west. So he walked softly before God, smothering his joy down under scowls and muttered curses, and, so, fooling God, for God was the only thing in the universe of which Dan Cullen was afraid.

All Saturday and Saturday night the *Mary Rogers* raced her westing. Persistently she logged her fourteen knots, so that by Sunday morning she had covered three hundred and fifty miles. If the wind held, she would make around. If it failed, and the snorter came from anywhere between south-west and north, back the *Mary Rogers* would be hurled and be no better off than she had been seven weeks before. And on Sunday morning the wind *was* failing. The big sea was going down and running smooth. Both watches were on deck setting sail after sail as fast as the ship could stand it. And now Captain Cullen went around brazenly before God, smoking a big cigar, smiling jubilantly, as if the failing wind delighted him, while down underneath he was raging against God for taking the life out of the blessed wind. *Make westing!* So he would, if God would only leave him alone. Secretly, he pledged himself anew to the Powers of Darkness, if they would let him make westing. He pledged himself so easily because he did not believe in the Powers of Darkness. He really believed only in God, though he did not know it. And in his inverted theology

God was really the Prince of Darkness. Captain Cullen was a devil-worshipper, but he called the devil by another name, that was all.

At midday, after calling eight bells, Captain Cullen ordered the royals on. The men went aloft faster than they had gone in weeks. Not alone were they nimble because of the westing, but a benignant sun was shining down and limbering their stiff bodies. George Dorety stood aft, near Captain Cullen, less bundled in clothes than usual, soaking in the grateful warmth as he watched the scene. Swiftly and abruptly the incident occurred. There was a cry from the foreroyal-yard of 'Man overboard!' Somebody threw a life-buoy over the side, and at the same instant the second's mate voice came aft, ringing and peremptory—

'Hard down your helm!'

The man at the wheel never moved a spoke. He knew better, for Captain Dan Cullen was standing alongside of him. He wanted to move a spoke, to move all the spokes, to grind the wheel down, hard down, for his comrade drowning in the sea. He glanced at Captain Dan Cullen, and Captain Dan Cullen gave no sign.

'Down! Hard down!' the second mate roared, as he sprang aft.

But he ceased springing and commanding, and stood still, when he saw Dan Cullen by the wheel. And big Dan Cullen puffed at his cigar and said nothing. Astern, and going astern fast, could be seen the sailor. He had caught the life-buoy and was clinging to it. Nobody spoke. Nobody moved. The men aloft clung to the royal-yards and watched with terror-stricken faces. And the *Mary Rogers* raced on, making her westing. A long, silent minute passed.

'Who was it?' Captain Cullen demanded.

'Mops, sir,' eagerly answered the sailor at the wheel.

Mops topped a wave astern and disappeared temporarily in the trough. It was a large wave, but it was no greybeard. A small boat could live easily in such a sea, and in such a sea the *Mary Rogers* could easily come to. But she could not come to and make westing at the same time.

For the first time in all his years, George Dorety was seeing a real drama of life and death—a sordid little drama in which the scales balanced an unknown sailor named Mops against a few miles longitude. At first he had watched the man astern but now he watched big Dan Cullen, hairy and black, vested with power of life and death, smoking a cigar.

Captain Dan Cullen smoked another long, silent minute. Then he removed the cigar from his mouth. He glanced aloft at the spars of the *Mary Rogers*, and overside at the sea.

'Sheet home the royals!' he cried.

Fifteen minutes later they sat at table, in the cabin, with food served before them. On one side of George Dorety sat Dan Cullen, the tiger, on the other side, Joshua Higgins, the hyena. Nobody spoke. On deck men were sheeting home the skysails. George Dorety could hear their cries, while a persistent vision haunted him of a man called Mops, alive and well, clinging to a life-buoy miles astern in that lonely ocean. He glanced at Captain Cullen, and experienced a feeling of nausea, for the man was eating his food with relish, almost bolting it.

'Captain Cullen,' Dorety said, 'you are in command of this ship, and it is not proper for me to comment now upon what you do. But I wish to say one thing. There is a hereafter, and yours will be a hot one.'

Captain Cullen did not even scowl. In his voice was regret as he said—

'It was blowing a living gale. It was impossible to save the man.'

'He fell from the royal-yard,' Dorety cried hotly. 'You were setting the royals at the time. Fifteen minutes afterwards you were setting the skysails.'

'It was a living gale, wasn't it, Mr. Higgins?' Captain Cullen said, turning to the mate.

'If you'd brought her to, it'd have taken the sticks out of her' was the mate's answer. 'You did the proper thing, Captain Cullen. The man hadn't a ghost of a show.'

George Dorety made no answer, and to the meal's end no one spoke. After that, Dorety had his meals served in his state-room. Captain Cullen scowled at him no longer, though no speech was exchanged between them, while the *Mary Rogers* sped north towards warmer latitudes. At the end of the week Dan Cullen cornered Dorety on deck.

'What are you going to do when we get to 'Frisco?' he demanded bluntly.

'I am going to swear out a warrant for your arrest,' Dorety answered quietly. 'I am going to charge you with murder, and I am going to see you hanged for it.'

'You're almighty sure of yourself,' Captain Cullen sneered, turning on his heel.

A second week passed, and one morning found George

Dorety standing in the coach-house companionway at the for'ard end of the long poop, taking his first gaze around the deck. The *Mary Rogers* was reaching full-and-by, in a stiff breeze. Every sail was set and drawing, including the staysails. Captain Cullen strolled for'ard along the poop. He strolled carelessly, glancing at the passenger out of the corner of his eye. Dorety was looking the other way, standing with head and shoulders outside the companionway, and only the back of his head was to be seen. Captain Cullen, with swift eye, embraced the mainstaysail-block and the head and estimated the distance. He glanced about him. Nobody was looking. Aft, Joshua Higgins, pacing up and down, had just turned his back and was going the other way. Captain Cullen bent over suddenly and cast the staysail-sheet off from its pin. The heavy block hurtled through the air, smashing Dorety's head like an egg-shell and hurtling on and back and forth as the staysail whipped and slatted in the wind. Joshua Higgins turned around to see what had carried away, and met the full blast of the vilest portion of Captain Cullen's profanity.

'I made the sheet fast myself,' whimpered the mate in the first lull, 'with an extra turn to make sure. I remember it distinctly.'

'Made fast?' the Captain snarled back, for the benefit of the watch as it struggled to capture the flying sail before it tore to ribbons. 'You couldn't make your grandmother fast, you useless hell's scullion. If you made that sheet fast with an extra turn, why in hell didn't it stay fast? That's what I want to know. Why in hell didn't it stay fast?'

The mate whined inarticulately.

'Oh, shut up!' was the final word of Captain Cullen.

Half an hour later he was as surprised as any when the body of George Dorety was found inside the companionway on the floor. In the afternoon, alone in his room, he doctored up the log.

'*Ordinary seaman, Karl Brun,*' he wrote, '*lost overboard from foreroyal-yard in a gale of wind. Was running at the time, and for the safety of the ship did not dare to come up the wind. Nor could a boat have lived in the sea that was running.*'

On another page he wrote:

'*Had often warned Mr. Dorety about the danger he ran because of his carelessness on deck. I told him, once, that some day he would get his head knocked off by a block. A carelessly fastened mainstay sailsheet was the cause of the accident, which was deeply to be regretted because Mr. Dorety was a favourite with all of us.*'

Captain Dan Cullen read over his literary effort with admiration, blotted the page, and closed the log. He lighted a cigar and stared before him. He felt the *Mary Rogers* lift, and heel, and surge along, and knew that she was making nine knots. A smile of satisfaction slowly dawned on his black and hairy face. Well, anyway, he had made his westing and fooled God.

The Madness of
John Harned

I tell this for a fact. It happened in the bull-ring at Quito. I sat in the box with John Harned, and with Maria Valenzuela, and with Luis Cervallos. I saw it happen. I saw it all from first to last. I was on the steamer *Ecuadore* from Panama to Guayaquil. Maria Valenzuela is my cousin. I have known her always. She is very beautiful. I am a Spaniard—an Ecuadoriano, true, but I am descended from Pedro Patino, who was one of Pizarro's captains. They were brave men. They were heroes. Did not Pizarro lead three hundred and fifty Spanish cavaliers and four thousand Indians into the far Cordilleras in search of treasure? And did not all the four thousand Indians and three hundred of the brave cavaliers die on that vain quest? But Pedro Patino did not die. He it was that lived to found the family of the Patino. I am Ecuadoriano, true, but I am Spanish. I am Manuel de Jesus Patino. I own many haciendas, and ten thousand Indians are my slaves, though the law says they are free men who work by freedom of contract. The law is a funny thing. We Ecuadorianos laugh at it. It is our law. We make it for ourselves. I am Manuel de Jesus Patino. Remember that name. It will be written some day in history. There are revolutions in Ecuador. We call them elections. It is a good joke is it not?—what you call a pun?

John Harned was an American. I met him first at the Tivoli Hotel in Panama. He had much money—this I have heard. He was going to Lima, but he met Maria Valenzuela in the Tivoli Hotel. Maria Valenzuela is my cousin, and she is beautiful. It is true, she is the most beautiful woman in Ecuador. But also is she most beautiful in every country—in Paris, in Madrid, in New York, in Vienna. Always do all men look at her, and John Harned looked long at her at Panama. He loved her, that I know for a fact. She was Ecuadoriano, true—but she was of all countries; she was of all the world. She spoke many languages. She sang—ah! like an artiste. Her smile—wonderful, divine. Her eyes—ah! have I not seen men look in her eyes? They were what you English call amazing. They were promises of paradise. Men drowned themselves in her eyes.

Maria Valenzuela was rich—richer than I, who am accounted very rich in Ecuador. But John Harned did not care for her money. He had a heart—a funny heart. He was a fool. He did not go to Lima. He left the steamer at Guayaquil and followed her to Quito. She was coming home from Europe and other places. I do not see what she found in him, but she liked him. This I know for a fact, else he would not have followed her to Quito. She asked him to come. Well do I remember the occasion. She said—

'Come to Quito and I will show you the bullfight—brave, clever, magnificent!'

But he said: 'I go to Lima, not Quito. Such is my passage engaged on the steamer.'

'You travel for pleasure—no?' said Maria Valenzuela; and she looked at him as only Maria Valenzuela could look, her eyes warm with the promise.

And he came. No; he did not come for the bull-fight. He came because of what he had seen in her eyes. Women like Maria Valenzuela are born once in a hundred years. They are of no country and no time. They are what you call universal. They are goddesses. Men fall down at their feet. They play with men and run them through their pretty fingers like sand. Cleopatra was such a woman they say: and so was Circe. She turned men into swine. Ha! ha! It is true—no?

It all came about because Maria Valenzuela said—

'You English people are—what shall I say?—savage—no? You prize-fight. Two men each hit the other with their fists till their eyes are blinded and their noses are broken. Hideous! And the other men who look on cry out loudly and are made glad. It is barbarous—no?'

'But they are men,' said John Harned; 'and they prize-fight

out of desire. No one makes them prize-fight. They do it because they desire it more than anything else in the world.'

Maria Valenzuela—there was scorn in her smile as she said—'They kill each other often—is it not so? I have read it in the papers.'

'But the bull,' said John Harned. 'The bull is killed many times in the bull-fight, and the bull does not come into the ring out of desire. It is not fair to the bull. He is compelled to fight. But the man in the prize-fight—no; he is not compelled.'

'He is the more brute therefore,' said Maria Valenzuela. 'He is savage. He is primitive. He is animal. He strikes with his paws like a bear from a cave, and he is ferocious. But the bull-fight—ah! You have not seen the bull-fight—no? The toreador is clever. He is only a man, soft and tender, and he faces the wild bull in conflict. And he kills with a sword, a slender sword, with one thrust, so, to the heart of the great beast. It is delicious. It makes the heart beat to behold—the small man, the great beast, the wide level sand, the thousands that look on without breath; the great beast rushes to the attack, the small man stands like a statue; he does not move, he is unafraid, and in his hand is the slender sword flashing like silver in the sun; nearer and nearer rushes the great beast with its sharp horns, the man does not move, and then—so—the sword flashes, the thrust is made, to the heart, to the hilt, the bull falls to the sand and is dead, and the man is unhurt. It is brave. It is magnificent! Ah!—I could love the toreador. But the man of the prize-fight—he is the brute, the human beast, the savage primitive, the maniac, that receives many blows in his stupid face and rejoices. Come to Quito and I will show you the brave sport, the sport of men, the toreador and the bull.'

But John Harned did not go to Quito for the bull-fight. He went because of Maria Valenzuela. He was a large man, more broad of shoulder than we Ecuadorianos, more tall, more heavy of limb and bone. True, he was larger even than most men of his own race. His eyes were blue, though I have seen them grey, and, sometimes, like cold steel. His features were large, too—not delicate like ours, and his jaw was very strong to look at. Also, his face was smooth-shaven like a priest's. Why should a man feel shame for the hair on his face? Did not God put it there? Yes, I believe in God. I am not a pagan like many of you English. God is good. He made me an Ecuadoriano with ten thousand slaves. And when I die I shall go to God. Yes, the priests are right.

But John Harned. He was a quiet man. He talked always in a

low voice, and he never moved his hands when he talked. One would have thought his heart was a piece of ice; yet did he have a streak of warm in his blood, for he followed Maria Valenzuela to Quito. Also, and for all that he talked low without moving his hands, he was an animal, as you shall see—the beast primitive, the stupid, ferocious savage of the long ago that dressed in wild skins and lived in the caves along with the bears and wolves.

Luis Cervallos is my friend, the best of Ecuadorianos. He owns three cacao plantations at Naranjito and Chobo. At Milagro is his big sugar plantation. He has large haciendas at Ambato and Latacunga, and down the coast is he interested in oil-wells. Also he has spent much money in planting rubber along the Guayas. He is modern, like the Yankee; and, like the Yankee, full of business. He had much money, but it is in many ventures, and ever he needs more money for new ventures and for the old ones. He has been everywhere and seen everything. When he was a very young man he was in the Yankee military academy what you call West Point. There was trouble. He was made to resign. He does not like Americans. But he did like Maria Valenzuela, who was of his own country. Also, he needed her money for his ventures and for his gold mine in eastern Ecuador where the painted Indians live. I was his friend. It was my desire that he should marry Maria Valenzuela. Further, much of my money had I invested in his ventures, more so in his gold mine which was very rich but which first required the expense of much money before it would yield forth its riches. If Luis Cervallos married Maria Valenzuela I should have more money very immediately.

But John Harned followed Maria Valenzuela to Quito and it was quickly clear to us—to Luis Cervallos and me—that she looked upon John Harned with great kindness. It is said that a woman will have her will, but this is a case not in point, for Maria Valenzuela did not have her will—at least not with John Harned. Perhaps it would all have happened as it did, even if Luis Cervallos and I had not sat in the box that day at the bull-ring in Quito. But this I know: we *did* sit in the box that day. And I shall tell you what happened.

The four of us were in the one box, guests of Luis Cervallos. It was next to the Presidente's box. On the other side was the box of General José Eliceo Salazar. With him were Joaquin Endara and Urcisino Castillo, both generals, and Colonel Jacinto Fierro and Captain Baltazar de Echeverria. Only Luis Cervallos had the position and influence to get that box next to the Presidente. I know for a fact that the Presidente himself expressed the desire to the management that Luis Cervallos should have that box.

The band finished playing the national hymn of Ecuador. The procession of the toreadors was over. The Presidente nodded to begin. The bugles blew, and the bull dashed in—you know the way, excited, bewildered, the darts in its shoulder burning like fire, itself seeking madly whatever enemy to destroy. The toreadors hid behind their shelters and waited. Suddenly they appeared forth, the capadors, five of them, from every side, their coloured capes flinging wide. The bull paused at sight of such generosity of enemies, unable in his own mind to know which to attack. Then advanced one of the capadors alone to meet the bull. The bull was very angry. With its forelegs it pawed the sand of the arena till the dust rose all about it. Then it charged, with lowered head, straight for the lone capador.

It is always of interest, the first charge of the first bull. After a time it is natural that one should grow tired, a trifle, that the keenness should lose its edge. But that first charge of the first bull! John Harned was seeing it for the first time, and he could not escape the excitement—the sight of the man, armed only with a piece of cloth, and of the bull rushing upon him across the sand with sharp horns, wide-spreading.

'See!' cried Maria Valenzuela. 'Is it not superb?'

John Harned nodded, but did not look at her. His eyes were sparkling, and they were only for the bull-ring. The capador stepped to the side, with a twirl of the cape eluding the bull and spreading the cape on his own shoulders.

'What do you think?' asked Maria Valenzuela. 'Is it not a —what-you-call—sporting proposition—no?'

'It is certainly,' said John Harned. 'It is very clever.'

She clapped her hands with delight. They were little hands. The audience applauded. The bull turned and came back. Again the capador eluded him, throwing the cape on his shoulders, and again the audience applauded. Three times did this happen. The capador was very excellent. Then he retired, and the other capadors played with the bull. After that they placed the banderillos in the bull, in the shoulders, on each side of the backbone, two at a time. Then stepped forward Ordonez, the chief matador, with the long sword and the scarlet cape. The bugles blew for the death. He is not so good as Matestini. Still he is good, and with one thrust he drove the sword to the heart, and the bull doubled his legs under him and lay down and died. It was a pretty thrust, clean and sure; and there was much applause, and many of the common people threw their hats into the ring. Maria Valenzuela clapped her hands with the rest, and John Harned, whose cold heart was not touched by the event, looked at her with curiosity.

'You like it?' he asked.

'Always,' she said, still clapping her hands.

'From a little girl,' said Luis Cervallos. 'I remember her first fight. She was four years old. She sat with her mother, and just like now she clapped her hands. She is a proper Spanish woman.'

'You have seen it,' said Maria Valenzuela to John Harned, as they fastened the mules to the dead bull and dragged it out. 'You have seen the bull-fight and you like it—no? What do you think?'

'I think the bull had no chance,' he said. 'The bull was doomed from the first. The issue was not in doubt. Every one knew, before the bull entered the ring, that it was to die. To be a sporting proposition, the issue must be in doubt. It was one stupid bull who had never fought a man against five wise men who had fought many bulls. It would be possibly a little bit fair if it were one man against one bull.'

'Or one man against five bulls,' said Maria Valenzuela; and we all laughed, and Luis Cervallos laughed loudest.

'Yes,' said John Harned, 'against five bulls, and the man, like the bulls, never in the bull-ring before—a man like yourself, Senor Cervallos.'

'Yet we Spanish like the bull-fight,' said Luis Cervallos; and I swear the devil was whispering then in his ear, telling him to do that which I shall relate.

'Then it must be a cultivated taste,' John Harned made answer. 'We kill bulls by the thousand every day in Chicago, yet no one cared to pay admittance to see.'

'That is butchery,' said I; 'but this—ah, this is an art. It is delicate. It is fine. It is rare.'

'Not always,' said Luis Cervallos. 'I have seen clumsy matadors, and I tell you it is not nice.'

He shuddered, and his face betrayed such what-you-call disgust, that I knew, then, that the devil was whispering and that he was beginning to play a part.

'Senor Harned may be right,' said Luis Cervallos. 'It may not be fair to the bull. For is it not known to all of us that for twenty-four hours the bull is given no water, and that immediately before the fight he is permitted to drink his fill?'

'And he comes into the ring heavy with water?' said John Harned quickly; and I saw that his eyes were very grey and very sharp and very cold.

'It is necessary for the sport,' said Luis Cervallos. 'Would you have the bull so strong that he would kill the toreadors?'

'I would that he had a fighting chance,' said John Harned, facing the ring to see the second bull come in.

It was not a good bull. It was frightened. It ran around the ring in search of a way to get out. The capadors stepped forth and flared their capes, but he refused to charge upon them.

'It is a stupid bull,' said Maria Valenzuela.

'I beg pardon,' said John Harned; 'but it would seem to me a wise bull. He knows he must not fight man. See! He smells death there in the ring.'

True. The bull, pausing where the last one had died, was smelling the wet sand and snorting. Again he ran around the ring, with raised head, looking at the faces of the thousands that hissed him, that threw orange-peel at him and called him names. But the smell of blood decided him and he charged a capador, so without warning that the man just escaped. He dropped his cape and dodged into the shelter. The bull struck the wall of the ring with a crash. And John Harned said, in a quiet voice, as though he talked to himself—

'I will give one thousand sucres to the lazar-house of Quito if a bull kills a man this day.'

'You like bulls?' said Maria Valenzuela with a smile.

'I like such men less,' said John Harned. 'A toreador is not a brave man. He surely cannot be a brave man. See, the bull's tongue is already out. He is tired and he has not yet begun.'

'It is the water,' said Luis Cervallos.

'Yes, it is the water,' said John Harned. 'Would it not be safer to hamstring the bull before he comes on?'

Maria Valenzuela was made angry by this sneer in John Harned's words. But Luis Cervallos smiled so that only I could see him, and then it broke upon my mind surely the game he was playing. He and I were to be banderilleros. The big American bull was there in the box with us. We were to stick the darts in him till he became angry, and then there might be no marriage with Maria Valenzuela. It was a good sport. And the spirit of bull-fighters was in our blood.

The bull was now angry and excited. The capadors had great game with him. He was very quick, and sometimes he turned with such sharpness that his hind legs lost their footing and he ploughed the sand with his quarter. But he charged always the flung capes and committed no harm.

'He has no chance,' said John Harned. 'He is fighting wind.'

'He thinks the cape is his enemy,' explained Maria Valenzuela. 'See how cleverly the capador deceives him.'

'It is his nature to be deceived,' said John Harned. 'Wherefore he is doomed to fight wind. The toreadors know it, the audience knows it, you know it, I know it—we all know from the first that he will fight wind. He only does not know it. It is his stupid beast-nature. He has no chance.'

'It is very simple,' said Luis Cervallos. 'The bull shuts his eyes when he charges. Therefore—'

'The man steps out of the way and the bull rushes by,' John Harned interrupted.

'Yes,' said Luis Cervallos; 'that is it. The bull shuts his eyes, and the man knows it.'

'But cows do not shut their eyes,' said John Harned. 'I know a cow at home that is a Jersey and gives milk, that would whip the whole gang of them.'

'But the toreadors do not fight cows,' said I.

'They are afraid to fight cows,' said John Harned.

'Yes,' said Luis Cervallos; 'they are afraid to fight cows. There would be no sport in killing toreadors.'

'There would be some sport,' said John Harned, 'if a toreador were killed once in a while. When I become an old man, and mayhap a cripple, and should I need to make a living and be unable to do hard work, then would I become a bull-fighter. It is a light vocation for elderly gentlemen and pensioners!'

'But see!' said Maria Valenzuela, as the bull charged bravely and the capador eluded it with a fling of his cape. 'It requires skill so to avoid the beast.'

'True,' said John Harned. 'But believe me, it requires a thousand times more skill to avoid the many and quick punches of a prize-fighter who keeps his eyes open and strikes with intelligence. Furthermore, this bull does not want to fight. Behold, he runs away.'

It was not a good bull, for again it ran around the ring, seeking to find a way out.

'Yet these bulls are sometimes the most dangerous,' said Luis Cervallos. 'It can never be known what they will do next. They are wise. They are half cow. The bull-fighters never like them. See! He has turned.'

Once again, baffled and made angry by the walls of the ring that would not let him out, the bull was attacking his enemies valiantly.

'His tongue is hanging out,' said John Harned. 'First, they fill him with water. Then they tire him out, one man and then another, persuading him to exhaust himself by fighting wind. While some tire him, others rest. But the bull they never let rest. Afterwards, when he is quite tired and no longer quick, the matador sticks the sword into him.'

The time had now come for the banderillos. Three times one of the fighters endeavoured to place the darts, and three times did he fail. He but stung the bull and maddened it. The banderillos must go in, you know, two at a time, into the shoulders, on each side the backbone and close to it. If but one be placed, it is a failure. The crowd hissed and called for Ordonez. And then Ordonez did a great thing. Four times he stood forth, and four times, at the first attempt, he stuck in the banderillos, so that eight of them, well placed, stood out of the back of the bull at one time. The crowd went mad, and a rain of hats and money fell upon the sand of the ring.

And just then the bull charged unexpectedly one of the capadors. The man slipped and lost his head. The bull caught him—fortunately, between his wide horns. And while the audience watched, breathless and silent, John Harned stood up and yelled with gladness. Alone, in that hush of all of us, John Harned yelled. And he yelled for the bull. As you see yourself, John Harned wanted the man killed. His was a brutal heart. This bad conduct made those angry that sat in the box of General Salazar, and they cried out against John Harned. And Urcisino Castillo told him to his face that he was a dog of a Gringo and other things. Only it was in Spanish, and John Harned did not understand. He stood and yelled, perhaps for the time of ten seconds, when the bull was enticed into charging the other capadors and the man arose unhurt.

'The bull has no chance,' John Harned said with sadness as he sat down. 'The man was uninjured. They fooled the bull away from him.' Then he turned to Maria Valenzuela and said: 'I beg your pardon. I was excited.'

She smiled and in reproof tapped his arm with her fan.

'It is your first bull-fight,' she cried. 'After you have seen more you will not cry for the death of the man. You Americans, you see, are more brutal than we. It is because of your prize-fighting. We come only to see the bull killed.'

'But I would the bull had some chance,' he answered.

'Doubtless, in time, I shall cease to be annoyed by the men who take advantage of the bull.'

The bugles blew for the death. Ordonez stood forth with the sword and the scarlet cloth. But the bull had changed again, and did not want to fight. Ordonez stamped his foot in the sand, and cried out, and waved the scarlet cloth. Then the bull charged, but without heart. There was no weight to the charge. It was a poor thrust. The sword struck a bone and bent. Ordonez took a fresh sword. The bull, again stung to fight, charged once more. Five times Ordonez essayed the thrust, and each time the sword went but part way in or struck bone. The sixth time, the sword went in to the hilt. But it was a bad thrust. The sword missed the heart and stuck out half a yard through the ribs on the opposite side. The audience hissed the matador. I glanced at John Harned. He sat silent, without movement; but I could see his teeth were set, and his hands were clenched tight on the railing of the box.

All fight was now out of the bull, and, though it was no vital thrust, he trotted lamely because of the sword that stuck through him, in one side and out the other. He ran away from the matador and the capadors, and circled the edge of the ring, looking up at the many faces.

'He is saying: "For God's sake let me out of this; I don't want to fight,"' said John Harned.

That was all. He said no more, but sat and watched, though sometimes he looked sideways at Maria Valenzuela to see how she took it. She was angry with the matador. He was awkward, and she had desired a clever exhibition.

The bull was now very tired, and weak from loss of blood, though far from dying. He walked slowly around the wall of the ring, seeking a way out. He would not charge. He had had enough. But he must be killed. There is a place, in the neck of a bull behind the horns, where the cord of the spine is un-protected and where a short stab will immediately kill. Ordonez stepped in front of the bull and lowered his scarlet cloth to the ground. The bull would not charge. He stood still and smelled the cloth, lowering his head to do so. Ordonez stabbed between the horns at the spot in the neck. The bull jerked his head up. The stab had missed. Then the bull watched the sword. When Ordonez moved the cloth on the ground, the bull forgot the sword and lowered his head to smell the cloth. Again Ordonez stabbed, and again he failed. He tried many times. It was stupid. And John Harned said nothing. At last a stab went home, and the bull fell to the sand, dead immediately, and the mules were made fast and he was dragged out.

'The Gringos say it is a cruel sport—no?' said Luis Cervallos. 'That it is not humane. That it is bad for the bull. No?'

'No,' said John Harned. 'The bull does not count for much. It is bad for those that look on. It is degrading to those that look on. It teaches them to delight in animal suffering. It is cowardly for five men to fight one stupid bull. Therefore those that look on learn to be cowards. The bull dies, but those that look on live and the lesson is learned. The bravery of men is not nourished by scenes of cowardice.'

Maria Valenzuela said nothing. Neither did she look at him. But she heard every word and her cheeks were white with anger. She looked out across the ring and fanned herself, but I saw that her hand trembled. Nor did John Harned look at her. He went on as though she were not there. He, too, was angry, coldly angry.

'It is the cowardly sport of a cowardly people,' he said.

'Ah,' said Luis Cervallos softly, 'you think you understand us.'

'I understand now the Spanish Inquisition,' said John Harned. 'It must have been more delightful than bull-fighting.'

Luis Cervallos smiled but said nothing. He glanced at Maria Valenzuela, and knew that the bull-fight in the box was won. Never would she have further to do with the Gringo who spoke such words. But neither Luis Cervallos nor I was prepared for the outcome of the day. I fear we do not understand the Gringos. How were we to know that John Harned, who was so coldly angry, should go suddenly mad? But mad he did go, as you shall see. The bull did not count for much—he said so himself. Then why should the horse count for so much? That I cannot understand. The mind of John Harned lacked logic. That is the only explanation.

'It is not usual to have horses in the bull-ring at Quito,' said Luis Cervallos, looking up from the programme. 'In Spain they always have them. But to-day, by special permission we shall have them. When the next bull comes on there will be horses and picadors—you know, the men who carry lances and ride the horses.'

'The bull is doomed from the first,' said John Harned. 'Are the horses then likewise doomed?'

'They are blindfolded so that they may not see the bull,' said Luis Cervallos. 'I have seen many horses killed. It is a brave sight.'

'I have seen the bull slaughtered,' said John Harned. 'I will now see the horse slaughtered, so that I may understand more fully the fine points of this noble sport.'

'They are old horses,' said Luis Cervallos, 'that are not good for anything else.'

'I see,' said John Harned.

The third bull came on, and soon against it were both capadors and picadors. One picador took his stand directly below us. I agree, it was a thin and aged horse he rode, a bag of bones covered with mangy hide.

'It is a marvel that the poor brute can hold up the weight of the rider,' said John Harned. 'And now that the horse fights the bull, what weapons has it?'

'The horse does not fight the bull,' said Luis Cervallos.

'Oh,' said John Harned, 'then is the horse there to be gored? That must be why it is blindfolded, so that it shall not see the bull coming to gore it.'

'Not quite so,' said I. 'The lance of the picador is to keep the bull from goring the horse.'

'Then are horses rarely gored?' asked John Harned.

'No,' said Luis Cervallos. 'I have seen, at Seville, eighteen horses killed in one day, and the people clamoured for more horses.'

'Were they blindfolded like this horse?' asked John Harned.

'Yes,' said Luis Cervallos.

After that we talked no more, but watched the fight. And John Harned was going mad all the time, and we did not know. The bull refused to charge the horse. And the horse stood still, and because it could not see it did not know that the capadors were trying to make the bull charge upon it. The capadors teased the bull with their capes, and when it charged them they ran towards the horse and into their shelters. At last the bull was well angry, and it saw the horse before it.

'The horse does not know, the horse does not know,' John Harned whispered like to himself, unaware that he voiced his thought aloud.

The bull charged, and of course the horse knew nothing till the picador failed and the horse found himself impaled on the bull's horns from beneath. The bull was magnificently strong. The sight of its strength was splendid to see. It lifted the horse clear into the air; and as the horse fell to its side on the ground the picador landed on his feet and escaped, while the capadors lured the bull away. The horse was emptied of its essential organs. Yet did it rise to its feet screaming. It was

the scream of the horse that did it, that made John Harned completely mad; for he, too, started to rise to his feet. I heard him curse low and deep. He never took his eyes from the horse, which, still screaming, strove to run, but fell down instead and rolled on its back so that all its four legs were kicking in the air. Then the bull charged it and gored it again and again until it was dead.

John Harned was now on his feet. His eyes were no longer cold like steel. They were blue flames. He looked at Maria Valenzuela, and she looked at him, and in his face was a great loathing. The moment of his madness was upon him. Everybody was looking, now that the horse was dead; and John Harned was a large man and easy to be seen.

'Sit down,' said Luis Cervallos, 'or you will make a fool of yourself.'

John Harned replied nothing. He struck out his fist. He smote Luis Cervallos in the face so that he fell like a dead man across the chairs and did not rise again. He saw nothing of what followed. But I saw much. Urcisino Castillo, leaning forward from the next box, with his cane struck John Harned full across the face. And John Harned smote him with his fist so that in falling he overthrew General Salazar. John Harned was now in what-you-call Berserker rage—no? The beast primitive in him was loose and roaring—the beast primitive of the holes and caves of the long ago.

'You came for a bull-fight,' I heard him say, 'and by God I'll show you a man-fight!'

It was a fight. The soldiers guarding the Presidente's box leaped across, but from one of them he took a rifle and beat them on their heads with it. From the other box Colonel Jacinto Fierro was shooting at him with a revolver. The first shot killed a soldier. This I know for a fact. I saw it. But the second shot struck John Harned in the side. Whereupon he swore, and with a lunge drove the bayonet of his rifle into Colonel Jacinto Fierro's body. It was horrible to behold. The Americans and the English are a brutal race. They sneer at our bull-fighting, yet do they delight in the shedding of blood. More men were killed that day because of John Harned than were ever killed in all the history of the bull-ring of Quito, yes, and of Guayaquil and all Ecuador.

It was the scream of the horse that did it. Yet why did not John Harned go mad when the bull was killed? A beast is a beast, be it bull or horse. John Harned was mad. There is no other explanation. He was blood-mad, a beast himself. I leave it to your judgment. Which is worse—the goring of the horse by the bull, or the goring of Colonel Jacinto Fierro by the bayonet in the hands of John Harned? And John Harned gored others with that bayonet. He was full of devils. He fought with many bullets in him, and he was hard to kill. And Marie Valenzuela was a brave woman. Unlike the other women, she did not cry out or faint. She sat still in her box, gazing out across the bull-ring. Her face was white and she fanned herself, but she never looked around.

From all sides came the soldiers and officers and the common people bravely to subdue the mad Gringo. It is true—the cry went up from the crowd to kill all the Gringos. It is an old cry in Latin-American countries, what of the dislike for the Gringos and their uncouth ways. It is true, the cry went up. But the brave Ecuadorianos killed only John Harned, and first he killed seven of them. Besides, there were many hurt. I have seen many bull-fights, but never have I seen anything so abominable as the scene in the boxes when the fight was over. It was like a field of battle. The dead lay around everywhere, while the wounded sobbed and groaned and some of them died. One man, whom John Harned had thrust through the belly with the bayonet, clutched at himself with both his hands and screamed. I tell you for a fact it was more terrible than the screaming of a thousand horses.

No, Maria Valenzuela did not marry Luis Cervallos. I am sorry for that. He was my friend, and much of my money was invested in his ventures. It was five weeks before the surgeons took the bandages from his face. And there is a scar there to this day, on the cheek, under the eye. Yet John Harned struck him but once and struck him only with his naked fist. Marie Valenzuela is in Austria now. It is said she is to marry an Archduke or some high nobleman. I do not know. I think she liked John Harned before he followed her to Quito to see the bull-fight. But why the horse? That is what I desire to know. Why should he watch the bull and say that it did not count, and then go immediately and most horribly mad because a horse screamed? There is no understanding the Gringos. They are barbarians.

A Piece of Steak

With the last morsel of bread Tom King wiped his plate clean of the last particle of flour gravy and chewed the resulting mouthful in a slow and meditative way. When he arose from the table, he was oppressed by the feeling that he was distinctly hungry. Yet he alone had eaten. The two children in the other room had been sent early to bed in order that in sleep they might forget they had gone supperless. His wife had touched nothing, and had sat silently and watched him with solicitous eyes. She was a thin, worn woman of the working class, though signs of an earlier prettiness were not wanting in her face. The flour for the gravy she had borrowed from the neighbour across the hall. The last two ha'pennies had gone to buy the bread.

He sat down by the window on a rickety chair that protested under his weight, and quite mechanically he put his pipe in his mouth and dipped into the side pocket of his coat. The absence of any tobacco made him aware of his action, and with a scowl for his forgetfulness he put the pipe away. His movements were slow, almost hulking, as though he were burdened by the heavy weight of his muscles. He was a solid-bodied, stolid-looking man, and his appearance did not suffer from being over-prepossessing. His rough clothes were old and slouchy. The uppers of his shoes were too weak to carry the heavy resoling that was itself of no recent date. And his cotton shirt, a cheap, two-shilling affair, showed a frayed collar and ineradicable paint stains.

But it was Tom King's face that advertised him unmistakably for what he was. It was the face of a typical prize-fighter; of one who had put in long years of service in the squared ring, and, by that means, developed and emphasized all the marks of the fighting beast. It was distinctly a lowering countenance, and, that no feature of it might escape notice, it was clean-shaven. The lips were shapeless and constituted a mouth harsh to excess, that was like a gash in his face. The jaw was aggressive, brutal, heavy. The eyes, slow of movement and heavy-lidded, were almost expressionless under the shaggy, indrawn brows. Sheer animal that he was, the eyes were the most animal-like feature about him. They were sleepy, lion-like—the eyes of a fighting animal. The forehead slanted quickly back to the hair, which, clipped close, showed every bump of a villainous-looking head. A nose, twice broken and moulded variously by countless blows, and a cauliflower ear, permanently swollen and distorted to twice its size, completed his adornment, while the beard, fresh-shaven as it was, sprouted in the skin and gave the face a blue-black stain.

Altogether, it was the face of a man to be afraid of in a dark alley or lonely place. And yet Tom King was not a criminal, nor had he ever done anything criminal. Outside of brawls, common to his walk in life, he had harmed no one. Nor had he ever been known to pick a quarrel. He was a professional, and all the fighting brutishness of him was reserved for his professional appearances. Outside the ring he was slow-going, easy-natured, and, in his younger days, when money was flush, too open-handed for his own good. He bore no grudges and had few enemies. Fighting was a business with him. In the ring he struck to hurt, struck to maim, struck to destroy; but there was no animus in it. It was a plain business proposition. Audiences assembled and paid for the spectacle of men knocking each other out. The winner took the big end of the purse. When Tom King faced the Woolloomoolloo Gouger, twenty years before, he knew that the Gouger's jaw was only four months healed after having been broken in a Newcastle bout. And he had played for that jaw and broken it again in the ninth round, not because he bore the Gouger any ill will, but because that was the surest way to put the Gouger out and win the big end of the purse. Nor had the Gouger borne him any ill will for it. It was the game, and both knew the game and played it.

A PIECE OF STEAK

Tom King had never been a talker, and he sat by the window, morosely silent, staring at his hands. The veins stood out on the backs of the hands, large and swollen; and the knuckles, smashed and battered and malformed, testified to the use to which they had been put. He had never heard that a man's life was the life of his arteries, but well he knew the meaning of those big, upstanding veins. His heart had pumped too much blood through them at top pressure. They no longer did the work. He had stretched the elasticity out of them, and with their distension had passed his endurance. He tired easily now. No longer could he do a fast twenty rounds, hammer and tongs, fight, fight, fight, from gong to gong, with fierce rally on top of fierce rally, beaten to the ropes and in turn beating his opponent to the ropes, and rallying fiercest and fastest of all in that last, twentieth round, with the house on its feet and yelling, himself rushing, striking, ducking, raining showers of blows upon showers of blows and receiving showers of blows in return, and all the time the heart faithfully pumping the surging blood through the adequate veins. The veins, swollen at the time, had always shrunk down again, though not quite—each time, imperceptibly at first, remaining just a trifle larger than before. He stared at them and at his battered knuckles, and, for the moment, caught a vision of the youthful excellence of those hands before the first knuckle had been smashed on the head of Benny Jones, otherwise known as the Welsh Terror.

The impression of his hunger came back on him.

'Blimey, but couldn't I go a piece of steak!' he muttered aloud, clenching his huge fists and spitting out a smothered oath.

'I tried both Burke's an' Sawley's,' his wife said half apologetically.

'An' they wouldn't?' he demanded.

'Not a ha'penny. Burke said——' She faltered.

'G'wan! Wot'd he say!'

'As how 'e was thinkin' Sandel 'ud do ye tonight, an' as how yer score was uncomfortable big as it was.'

Tom King grunted but did not reply. He was busy thinking of the bull terrier he had kept in his younger days to which he had fed steaks without end. Burke would have given him credit for a thousand steaks—then. But times had changed. Tom King was getting old; and old men, fighting before second-rate clubs, couldn't expect to run bills of any size with the tradesmen.

He had got up in the morning with a longing for a piece of steak, and the longing had not abated. He had not had a fair training for this fight. It was a drought year in Australia, times were hard, and even the most irregular work was difficult to find. He had had no sparring partner, and his food had not been of the best nor always sufficient. He had done a few days' navvy work when he could get it, and he had run around the Domain in the early mornings to get his legs in shape. But it was hard, training without a partner and with a wife and two kiddies that must be fed. Credit with the tradesmen had undergone very slight expansion when he was matched with Sandel. The secretary of the Gayety Club had advanced him three pounds —the loser's end of the purse—and beyond that had refused to go. Now and again he had managed to borrow a few shillings from old pals, who would have lent more only that it was a drought year and they were hard put themselves. No—and there was no use in disguising the fact—his training had not been satisfactory. He should have had better food and no worries. Besides, when a man is forty, it is harder to get into condition than when he is twenty.

'What time is it, Lizzie?' he asked.

His wife went across the hall to inquire, and came back.

'Quarter before eight.'

'They'll be startin' the first bout in a few minutes,' he said 'Only a try-out. Then there's a four-round spar 'tween Dealer Wells an' Gridley, an' a ten-round go 'tween Starlight an' some sailor bloke. I don't come on for over an hour.'

At the end of another silent ten minutes he rose to his feet.

'Truth is, Lizzie, I ain't had proper trainin'.'

He reached for his hat and started for the door. He did not offer to kiss her—he never did on going out—but on this night she dared to kiss him, throwing her arms around him and compelling him to bend down to her face. She looked quite small against the massive bulk of the man.

'Good luck, Tom,' she said. 'You gotter do 'im.'

'Ay, I gotter do 'im,' he repeated. 'That's all there is to it. I jus' gotter do 'im.'

He laughed with an attempt at heartiness, while she pressed more closely against him. Across her shoulders he looked around the bare room. It was all he had in the world, with the rent overdue, and her and the kiddies. And he was leaving it to go out into the night to get meat for his mate and cubs— not like a modern working-man going to his machine grind, but in the old, primitive, royal, animal way, by fighting for it.

'I gotter do 'im,' he repeated, this time a hint of desperation in his voice. 'If it's a win, it's thirty quid—and I can pay all that's owin', with a lump o' money left over. If it's a lose, I get naught—not even a penny for me to ride home on the tram. The secretary's give all that's comin' from a loser's end. Good-bye, old woman. I'll come straight home if it's a win.'

'An' I'll be waitin' up,' she called to him along the hall.

It was a full two miles to the Gayety, and as he walked along he remembered how in his palmy days—he had once been the heavyweight champion of New South Wales—he would have ridden in a cab to the fight, and how, most likely, some heavy backer would have paid for the cab and ridden with him. There were Tommy Burns and that Yankee, Jack Johnson—they rode about in motor-cars. And he walked! And, as any man knew, a hard two miles was not the best preliminary to a fight. He was an old 'un, and the world did not wag well with old 'uns. He was good for nothing now except navvy work, and his broken nose and swollen ear were against him even in that. He found himself wishing that he had learned a trade. It would have been better in the long run. But no one had told him, and he knew, deep down in his heart, that he would not have listened if they had. It had been so easy. Big money— sharp, glorious fights—periods of rest and loafing in between —a following of eager flatterers, the slaps on the back, the shakes of the hand, the toffs glad to buy him a drink for the privilege of five minutes' talk—and the glory of it, the yelling houses, the whirlwind finish, the referee's 'King wins!' and his name in the sporting columns next day.

Those had been times! But he realized now, in his slow, ruminating way, that it was the old 'uns he had been putting away. He was Youth, rising; and they were Age, sinking. No wonder it had been easy—they with their swollen veins and battered knuckles and weary in the bones of them from the long battles they had already fought. He remembered the time he put out old Stowsher Bill, at Rush-Cutters Bay, in the eighteenth round, and how old Bill had cried afterwards in the dressing-room like a baby. Perhaps old Bill's rent had been overdue. Perhaps he'd had at home a missus an' a couple of kiddies. And perhaps Bill, that very day of the fight, had had a hungering for a piece of steak. Bill had fought game and taken incredible punishment. He could see now, after he had gone through the mill himself, that Stowsher Bill had fought for a bigger stake, that night twenty years ago, than had young Tom King, who had fought for glory and easy money. No wonder Stowsher Bill had cried afterwards in the dressing-room.

Well, a man had only so many fights in him, to begin with.

It was the iron law of the game. One man might have a hundred hard fights in him, another man only twenty; each, according to the make of him and the quality of his fibre, had a definite number, and when he had fought them he was done. Yes, he had had more fights in him than most of them, and he had had far more than his share of the hard, gruelling fights—the kind that worked the heart and lungs to bursting, that took the elastic out of the arteries and made hard knots of muscle out of youth's sleek suppleness, that wore out nerve and stamina and made brain and bones weary from excess of effort and endurance overwrought. Yes, he had done better than all of them. There was none of his old fighting partners left. He was the last of the old guard. He had seen them all finished, and he had had a hand in finishing some of them.

They had tried him out against the old 'uns, and one after another he had put them away—laughing when, like old Stowsher Bill, they cried in the dressing-room. And now he was an old 'un, and they tried out the youngsters on him. There was that bloke Sandel. He had come over from New Zealand with a record behind him. But nobody in Australia knew anything about him, so they put him up against old Tom King. If Sandel made a showing, he would be given better men to fight, with bigger purses to win; so it was to be depended upon that he would put up a fierce battle. He had everything to win by it—money and glory and career; and Tom King was the grizzled old chopping block that guarded the highway to fame and fortune. And he had nothing to win except thirty quid, to pay to the landlord and the tradesmen. And as Tom King thus ruminated, there came to his stolid vision the form of youth, glorious youth, rising exultant and invincible, supple of muscle and silken of skin, with heart and lungs that had never been tired and torn and that laughed at limitation of effort. Yes, youth was the nemesis. It destroyed the old 'uns and recked not that, in so doing, it destroyed itself. It enlarged its arteries and smashed its knuckles, and was in turn destroyed by youth. For youth was ever youthful. It was only age that grew old.

At Castlereagh Street he turned to the left, and three blocks along came to the Gayety. A crowd of young larrikins hanging outside the door made respectful way for him, and he heard one say to another: 'That's 'im! That's Tom King!'

Inside, on the way to his dressing-room, he encountered the secretary, a keen-eyed, shrewd-faced young man, who shook his hand.

A PIECE OF STEAK

'How are you feelin', Tom?' he asked.

'Fit as a fiddle,' King answered, though he knew that he lied, and that if he had a quid he would give it right there for a good piece of steak.

When he emerged from the dressing-room, his seconds behind him, and came down the aisle to the squared ring in the centre of the hall, a burst of greeting and applause went up from the waiting crowd. He acknowledged salutations right and left, though few of the faces did he know. Most of them were the faces of kiddies unborn when he was winning his first laurels in the squared ring. He leaped lightly to the raised platform and ducked through the ropes to his corner, where he sat down on a folding stool. Jack Ball, the referee, came over and shook his hand. Ball was a broken-down pugilist who for over ten years had not entered the ring as a principal. King was glad that he had him for referee. They were both old 'uns. If he should rough it with Sandel a bit beyond the rules, he knew Ball could be depended upon to pass it by.

Aspiring young heavyweights, one after another, were climbing into the ring and being presented to the audience by the referee. Also he issued their challenges for them.

'Young Pronto,' Bill announced, 'from North Sydney, challenges the winner for fifty pounds side bet.'

The audience applauded, and applauded again as Sandel himself sprang through the ropes and sat down in his corner. Tom King looked across the ring at him curiously, for in a few minutes they would be locked together in merciless combat, each trying with all the force of him to knock the other into unconsciousness. But little could he see, for Sandel, like himself, had trousers and sweater on over his ring costume. His face was strongly handsome, crowned with a curly mop of yellow hair, while his thick, muscular neck hinted at bodily magnificence.

Young Pronto went to one corner and then the other, shaking hands with the principals and dropping down out of the ring. The challenges went on. Ever youth climbed through the ropes—youth unknown but insatiable, crying out to mankind that with strength and skill it would match issues with the winner. A few years before, in his own hey-day of invincibleness, Tom King would have been amused and bored by these preliminaries. But now he sat fascinated, unable to shake the vision of youth from his eyes. Always were these youngsters rising up in the boxing game, springing through the ropes and shouting their defiance; and always were the old 'uns going down before them. They climbed to success over the bodies of the old 'uns. And ever they came, more and more youngsters—youth unquenchable and irresistible—and ever they put the old 'uns away, themselves becoming old 'uns and travelling the same downward path, while behind them, ever pressing on them, was youth eternal—the new babies, grown lusty and dragging their elders down, with behind them more babies to the end of time—youth that must have its will and that will never die.

King glanced over to the press box, nodded to Morgan, of the *Sportsman*, and Corbett, of the *Referee*. Then he held out his hands, while Sid Sullivan and Charley Bates, his seconds, slipped on his gloves and laced them tight, closely watched by one of Sandel's seconds, who first examined critically the tapes on King's knuckles. A second of his own was in Sandel's corner, performing a like office. Sandel's trousers were pulled off, and as he stood up his sweater was skinned off over his head. And Tom King, looking, saw youth incarnate, deep-chested, heavy-thewed, with muscles that slipped and slid like live things under the white satin skin. The whole body was acrawl with life, and Tom King knew that it was a life that had never oozed its freshness out through the aching pores during the long fights wherein youth paid its toll and departed not quite so young as when it entered.

The two men advanced to meet each other, and as the gong sounded and the seconds clattered out of the ring with the folding stools, they shook hands and instantly took their fighting attitudes. And instantly, like a mechanism of steel and springs balanced on a hair trigger, Sandel was in and out and in again, landing a left to the eyes, a right to the ribs, ducking a counter, dancing lightly away and dancing menacingly back again. He was swift and clever. It was a dazzling exhibition. The house yelled its approbation. But King was not dazzled. He had fought too many fights and too many youngsters. He knew the blows for what they were—too quick and too deft to be dangerous. Evidently Sandel was going to rush things from the start. It was to be expected. It was the way of youth, expending its splendour and excellence in wild insurgence and furious onslaught, overwhelming opposition with its own unlimited glory of strength and desire.

Sandel was in and out, here, there, and everywhere, light-footed and eager-hearted, a living wonder of white flesh and stinging muscle that wove itself into a dazzling fabric of attack, slipping and leaping like a flying shuttle from action to action through a thousand actions, all of them centred upon the destruction of Tom King, who stood between him and fortune. And Tom King patiently endured. He knew his business, and he knew youth now that youth was no longer his. There was nothing to do till the other lost some of his steam, was his thought, and he grinned to himself as he deliberately ducked so as to receive a heavy blow on the top of his head. It was a wicked thing to do, yet eminently fair according to the rules of the boxing game. A man was supposed to take care of his own knuckles, and if he insisted on hitting an opponent on the top of the head he did so at his own peril. King could have ducked lower and let the blow whizz harmlessly past, but he remembered his own early fights and how he smashed his first knuckle on the head of the Welsh Terror. He was but playing the game. That duck had accounted for one of Sandel's knuckles. Not that Sandel would mind it now. He would go on, superbly regardless, hitting as hard as ever throughout the fight. But later on, when the long ring battles had begun to tell, he would regret that knuckle and look back and remember how he smashed it on Tom King's head.

The first round was all Sandel's, and he had the house yelling with the rapidity of his whirlwind rushes. He overwhelmed King with avalanches of punches, and King did nothing. He never struck once, contenting himself with covering up, blocking and ducking and clinching to avoid punishment. He occasionally feinted, shook his head when the weight of a punch landed, and moved stolidly about, never leaping or springing or wasting an ounce of strength. Sandel must foam the froth of youth away before discreet age could dare to retaliate. All King's movements were slow and methodical, and his heavy-lidded, slow-moving eyes gave him the appearance of being half asleep or dazed. Yet they were eyes that saw everything, that had been trained to see everything through all his twenty years and odd in the ring. They were eyes that did not blink or waver before an impending blow, but that coolly saw and measured distance.

Seated back in his corner for the minute's rest at the end of the round, he lay back with outstretched legs, his arms resting on the right-angle of the ropes, his chest and abdomen heaving frankly and deeply as he gulped down the air driven by the towels of his seconds. He listened with closed eyes to the voices of the house, 'Why don't yeh fight, Tom?' many were crying. 'Yeh ain't afraid of 'im, are yeh?'

'Muscle-bound,' he heard a man on a front seat comment. 'He can't move quicker. Two to one on Sandels, in quids.'

The gong struck and the two men advanced from their corners. Sandel came forward fully three-quarters of the distance, eager to begin again; but King was content to advance the shorter distance. It was in line with his policy of economy. He had not been well trained, and he had not had enough to eat, and every step counted. Besides, he had already walked two miles to the ringside. It was a repetition of the first round, with Sandel attacking like a whirlwind and with the audience indignantly demanding why King did not fight. Beyond feinting and several slowly delivered and ineffectual blows he did nothing save block and stall and clinch. Sandel wanted to make the pace fast, while King, out of his wisdom, refused to accommodate him. He grinned with a certain wistful pathos in his ring-battered countenance, and went on cherishing his strength with the jealousy of which only age is capable. Sandel was youth, and he threw his strength away with the munificent abandon of youth. To King belonged the ring generalship, the wisdom bred of long, aching fights. He watched with cool eyes and head, moving slowly and waiting for Sandel's froth to foam away. To the majority of the onlookers it seemed as though King was hopelessly outclassed, and they voiced their opinion in offers of three to one on Sandel. But there were wise ones, a few, who knew King of old time, and who covered what they considered easy money.

The third round began as usual, one-sided, with Sandel doing all the leading and delivering all the punishment. A half minute had passed when Sandel, over-confident, left an opening. King's eyes and right arm flashed in the same instant. It was his first real blow—a hook, with the twisted arch of the arm to make it rigid, and with all the weight of the half-pivoted body behind it. It was like a sleepy-seeming lion suddenly thrusting out a lightning paw. Sandel, caught on the side of the jaw, was felled like a bullock. The audience gasped and murmured awe-stricken applause. The man was not muscle-bound, after all, and he could drive a blow like a trip hammer.

Sandel was shaken. He rolled over and attempted to rise, but the sharp yells from his seconds to take the count restrained him. He knelt on one knee, ready to rise, and waited, while the referee stood over him, counting the seconds loudly in his ear. At the ninth he rose in fighting attitude, and Tom King, facing him, knew regret that the blow had not been an inch nearer the point of the jaw. That would have been a knock-out, and he could have carried the thirty quid home to the missus and the kiddies.

The round continued to the end of its three minutes, Sandel for the first time respectful of his opponent and King slow of movement and sleepy-eyed as ever. As the round neared its close, King, warned of the fact by sight of the seconds crouching outside ready for the spring in through the ropes, worked the fight around to his own corner. And when the gong struck, he sat down immediately on the waiting stool, while Sandel had to walk all the way across the diagonal of the square to his own corner. It was a little thing, but it was the sum of little things that counted. Sandel was compelled to walk that many more steps, to give up that much energy, and to lose a part of the precious minute of rest. At the beginning of every round King loafed slowly out from his corner, forcing his opponent to advance the greater distance. The end of every round found the fight manœuvred by King into his own corner so that he could immediately sit down.

Two more rounds went by, in which King was parsimonious of effort and Sandel prodigal. The latter's attempt to force a fast pace made King uncomfortable, for a fair percentage of the multitudinous blows showered upon him went home. Yet King persisted in his dogged slowness, despite the crying of the young hotheads for him to go in and fight. Again, in the sixth round, Sandel was careless, again Tom King's fearful right flashed out to the jaw, and again Sandel took the nine seconds' count.

By the seventh round Sandel's pink of condition was gone, and he settled down to what he knew was to be the hardest fight in his experience. Tom King was an old 'un, but a better old 'un than he had ever encountered—an old 'un who never lost his head, who was remarkably able at defence, whose blows had the impact of a knotted club, and who had a knock-out in either hand. Nevertheless, Tom King dared not hit often. He never forgot his battered knuckles, and knew that every hit must count if the knuckles were to last out the fight. As he sat in his corner, glancing across at his opponent, the thought came to him that the sum of his wisdom and Sandel's youth would constitute a world's champion heavyweight. But that was the trouble. Sandel would never become a world champion. He lacked the wisdom, and the only way for him to get it was to buy it with youth; and when wisdom was his, youth would have been spent in buying it.

King took every advantage he knew. He never missed an

opportunity to clinch, and in effecting most of the clinches his shoulder drove stiffly into the other's ribs. In the philosophy of the ring a shoulder was as good a punch so far as damage was concerned, and a great deal better so far as concerned expenditure of effort. Also in the clinches King rested his weight on his opponent, and was loath to let go. This compelled the interference of the referee, who tore them apart, always assisted by Sandel who had not yet learned to rest. He could not refrain from using those glorious flying arms and writhing muscles of his, and when the other rushed into a clinch, striking shoulder against ribs, and with head resting under Sandel's left arm, Sandel almost invariably swung his right behind his own back and into the projecting face. It was a clever stroke, much admired by the audience, but it was not dangerous, and was, therefore, just that much wasted strength. But Sandel was tireless and unaware of limitations, and King grinned and doggedly endured.

Sandel developed a fierce right to the body, which made it appear that King was taking an enormous amount of punishment, and it was only the old ringsters who appreciated the deft touch of King's left glove to the other's biceps just before the impact of the blow. It was true, the blow landed each time; but each time it was robbed of its power by that touch on the biceps. In the ninth round, three times inside a minute, King's right hooked its twisted arch to the jaw; and three times Sandel's body, heavy as it was, was levelled to the mat. Each time he took the nine seconds allowed him and rose to his feet, shaken and jarred, but still strong. He had lost much of his speed, and he wasted less effort. He was fighting grimly; but he continued to draw upon his chief asset, which was youth. King's chief asset was experience. As his vitality had dimmed and his vigour abated, he had replaced them with cunning, with wisdom born of the long fights and with a careful shepherding of strength. Not alone had he learned never to make a superfluous movement, but he had learned how to seduce an opponent into throwing his strength away. Again and again, by feint of foot and hand and body, he continued to inveigle Sandel into leaping back, ducking, or countering. King rested, but he never permitted Sandel to rest. It was the strategy of age.

Early in the tenth round King began stopping the other's rushes with straight lefts to the face, and Sandel, grown wary, responded by drawing the left, then by ducking it and delivering his right in a swinging hook to the side of the head. It was too high up to be vitally effective; but when it first landed King knew the old, familiar descent of the black veil of unconsciousness across his mind. For the instant, or for the slightest fraction of an instant, rather, he ceased. In the one moment he saw his opponent ducking out of his field of vision and the background of white, watching faces; in the next moment he again saw his opponent and the background of faces. It was as if he had slept for a time and just opened his eyes again, and yet the interval of unconsciousness was so microscopically short that there had been no time for him to fall. The audience saw him totter and his knees hive, and then saw him recover and tuck his chin deeper into the shelter of his left shoulder.

Several times Sandel repeated the blow, keeping King partially dazed, and then the latter worked out his defence, which was also a counter. Feinting with his left, he took a half step backward, at the same time uppercutting with the whole strength of his right. So accurately was it timed that it landed squarely on Sandel's face in the full, downward sweep of the duck, and Sandel lifted in the air and curled backwards, striking the mat on his head and shoulders. Twice King achieved this, then turned loose and hammered his opponent to the ropes. He gave Sandel no chance to rest or to set himself, but smashed blow in upon blow till the house rose to its feet and the air was filled with an unbroken roar of applause. But Sandel's strength and endurance were superb, and he continued to stay on his feet. A knock-out seemed certain, and a captain of police, appalled at the dreadful punishment, arose by the ringside to stop the fight. The gong struck for the end of the round and Sandel staggered to his corner, protesting to the captain that he was sound and strong. To prove it, he threw two back air-springs, and the police captain gave in.

Tom King, leaning back in his corner and breathing hard, was disappointed. If the fight had been stopped, the referee, perforce, would have rendered him the decision and the purse would have been his. Unlike Sandel, he was not fighting for glory or career, but for thirty quid. And now Sandel would recuperate in the minute of rest.

Youth will be served—this saying flashed into King's mind, and he remembered the first time he had heard it, the night when he had put away Stowsher Bill. The toff who had bought him a drink after the fight and patted him on the shoulder had used those words. Youth will be served! The toff was right. And on that night in the long ago he had been youth. Tonight youth sat in the opposite corner. As for himself, he had been fighting for half an hour now, and he was an old man. Had he fought like Sandel, he would not have lasted fifteen minutes. But the point was that he did not recuperate. Those upstanding arteries and that sorely tried heart would not enable him to gather strength in the intervals between the rounds. And he had not had sufficient strength in him to begin with. His legs were heavy under him and beginning to cramp. He should not have walked those two miles to the fight. And there was the steak which he had got up longing for that morning. A great and terrible hatred rose up in him for the butchers who had refused him credit. It was hard for an old man to go into a fight without enough to eat. And a piece of steak was such a little thing, a few pennies at best; yet it meant thirty quid to him.

With the gong that opened the eleventh round Sandel rushed, making a show of freshness which he did not really possess. King knew it for what it was—a bluff as old as the game itself. He clinched to save himself, then, going free, allowed Sandel to get set. This was what King desired. He feinted with his left, drew the answering duck and swinging upward hook, then made the half step backward, delivered the uppercut full to the face and crumpled Sandel over to the mat. After that he never let him rest, receiving punishment himself, but inflicting far more, smashing Sandel to the ropes, hooking and driving all manner of blows into him, tearing away from his clinches or punching him out of attempted clinches, and ever when Sandel would have fallen, catching him with one uplifting hand and with the other immediately smashing him into the ropes where he could not fall.

The house by this time had gone mad, and it was his house, nearly every voice yelling: 'Go it, Tom!' 'Get 'im! Get 'im!' 'You've got 'im, Tom! You've got 'im!' It was to be a whirlwind finish, and that was what a ringside audience paid to see.

And Tom King, who for half an hour had conserved his strength, now expended it prodigally in the one great effort he knew he had in him. It was his one chance—now or not at all. His strength was waning fast, and his hope was that before the last of it ebbed out of him he would have beaten his opponent down for the count. And as he continued to strike and force, coolly estimating the weight of his blows and the quality of the damage wrought, he realized how hard a man Sandel was to knock out. Stamina and endurance were his to an extreme degree, and they were the virgin stamina and endurance of youth. Sandel was certainly a coming man. He had it in him. Only out of such rugged fibre were successful fighters fashioned.

Sandel was reeling and staggering, but Tom King's legs were cramping and his knuckles going back on him. Yet he steeled himself to strike the fierce blows, every one of which brought anguish to his tortured hands. Though now he was receiving practically no punishment, he was weakening as rapidly as the other. His blows went home, but there was no longer the weight behind them, and each blow was the result of a severe effort of will. His legs were like lead, and they dragged visibly under him; while Sandel's backers, cheered by this symptom, began calling encouragement to their man.

King was spurred to a burst of effort. He delivered two blows in succession—a left, a trifle too high, to the solar plexus, and a right cross to the jaw. They were not heavy blows, yet so weak and dazed was Sandel that he went down and lay quivering. The referee stood over him, shouting the count of the fatal seconds in his ear. If before the tenth second was called he did not rise, the fight was lost. The house stood in hushed silence. King rested on trembling legs. A mortal dizziness was upon him, and before his eyes the sea of faces sagged and swayed, while to his ears, as from a remote distance, came the count of the referee. Yet he looked upon the fight as his. It was impossible that a man so punished could rise.

Only youth could rise, and Sandel rose. At the fourth second he rolled over on his face and groped blindly for the ropes. By the seventh second he had dragged himself to his knee, where he rested, his head rolling groggily on his shoulders. As the referee cried 'Nine!' Sandel stood upright, in proper stalling position, his left arm wrapped about his face, his right wrapped about his stomach. Thus were his vital points guarded, while he lurched towards King in the hope of effecting a clinch and gaining more time.

At the instant Sandel arose, King was at him, but the two blows he delivered were muffled on the stalled arms. The next moment Sandel was in the clinch and holding on desperately while the referee strove to drag the two men apart. King helped to force himself free. He knew the rapidity with which youth recovered, and he knew that Sandel was his if he could prevent that recovery. One stiff punch would do it. Sandel was his, indubitably his. He had outgeneralled him, outfought him, outpointed him. Sandel reeled out of the clinch, balanced on the hairline between defeat or survival. One good blow would topple him over and down and out. And Tom King, in a flash of bitterness, remembered the piece of steak and wished that he had it then behind that necessary punch he must deliver. He nerved himself for the blow, but it was not heavy enough nor swift enough. Sandel swayed but did not fall, staggering back to the ropes and holding on. King staggered after him, and, with a pang like that of dissolution, delivered another blow. But his body had deserted him. All that was left of him was a fighting intelligence that was dimmed and clouded from exhaustion. The blow that was aimed for the jaw struck no higher than the shoulder. He had willed the blow higher, but the tired muscles had not been able to obey. And, from the impact of the blow, Tom King himself reeled back and nearly fell. Once again he strove. This time his punch missed altogether, and from absolute weakness he fell against Sandel and clinched, holding on to him to save himself from sinking to the floor.

King did not attempt to free himself. He had shot his bolt. He was gone. And youth had been served. Even in the clinch he could feel Sandel growing stronger against him. When the referee thrust them apart, there, before his eyes, he saw youth recuperate. From instant to instant Sandel grew stronger. His punches, weak and futile at first, became stiff and accurate. Tom King's bleared eyes saw the gloved fist driving at his jaw, and he willed to guard it by interposing his arm. He saw the danger, willed the act; but the arm was too heavy. It seemed burdened with a hundredweight of lead. It would not lift itself, and he strove to lift it with his soul. Then the gloved fist landed home. He experienced a sharp snap that was like an electric spark, and simultaneously the veil of blackness enveloped him.

When he opened his eyes again he was in his corner, and he heard the yelling of the audience like the roar of the surf at Bondi Beach. A wet sponge was being pressed against the base of his brain, and Sid Sullivan was blowing cold water in a refreshing spray over his face and chest. His gloves had already been removed, and Sandel, bending over him, was shaking his hand. He bore no ill will towards the man who had put him out, and he returned the grip with a heartiness that made his battered knuckles protest. Then Sandel stepped to the centre of the ring and the audience hushed its pandemonium to hear him accept young Pronto's challenge and offer to increase the side bet to one hundred pounds. King looked on apathetically while his seconds mopped the streaming water from him, dried his face, and prepared him to leave the ring. He felt hungry. It was not the ordinary, gnawing kind, but a great faintness, a palpitation at the pit of the stomach that communicated itself to all his body. He remembered back into the fight to the moment when he had Sandel swaying and tottering on the hairline balance of defeat. Ah, that piece of steak would have done it! He had lacked just that for the decisive blow, and he had lost. It was all because of the piece of steak.

His seconds were half supporting him as they helped him through the ropes. He tore free from them, ducked through the ropes unaided, and leaped heavily to the floor, following on their heels as they forced a passage for him down the crowded centre aisle. Leaving the dressing-room for the street, in the entrance to the hall, some young fellow spoke to him.

'W'y didn't yuh go in an' get 'im when yuh 'ad 'im?' the young fellow asked.

'Aw, go to hell!' said Tom King, and passed down the steps to the sidewalk.

The doors of the public house at the corner were swinging wide, and he saw the lights and the smiling barmaids, heard the many voices discussing the fight and the prosperous chink of money on the bar. Somebody called to him to have a drink. He hesitated perceptibly, then refused and went on his way.

He had not a copper in his pocket, and the two-mile walk home seemed very long. He was certainly getting old. Crossing the Domain he sat down suddenly on a bench, unnerved by the thought of the missus sitting up for him, waiting to learn the outcome of the fight. That was harder than any knock-out, and it seemed almost impossible to face.

He felt weak and sore, and the pain of his smashed knuckles warned him that, even if he could find a job at navvy work, it would be a week before he could grip a pick handle or a shovel. The hunger palpitation at the pit of the stomach was sickening. His wretchedness overwhelmed him, and into his eyes came an unwonted moisture. He covered his face with his hands, and, as he cried, he remembered Stowsher Bill and how he had served him that night in the long ago. Poor old Stowsher Bill! He could understand now why Bill had cried in the dressing-room.

The Terrible Solomons

There is no gainsaying that the Solomons are a hard-bitten bunch of islands. On the other hand, there are worse places in the world. But to the new chum who has no constitutional understanding of men and life in the rough, the Solomons may indeed prove terrible.

It is true that fever and dysentery are perpetually on the walk-about, that loathsome skin diseases abound, that the air is saturated with a poison that bites into every pore, cut, or abrasion and plants malignant ulcers, and that many strong men who escape dying there return as wrecks to their own countries. It is also true that the natives of the Solomons are a wild lot, with a hearty appetite for human flesh and a fad for collecting human heads. Their highest instinct of sportsman-ship is to catch a man with his back turned and to smite him a cunning blow with a tomahawk that severs the spinal column at the base of the brain. It is equally true that on some islands, such as Malaita, the profit and loss account of social inter-course is calculated in homicides. Heads are a medium of ex-change, and white heads are extremely valuable. Very often a dozen villages make a jack-pot, which they fatten moon by moon, against the time when some brave warrior presents a white man's head, fresh and gory, and claims the pot.

All the foregoing is quite true, and yet there are white men who have lived in the Solomons a score of years and who feel homesick when they go away from them. A man needs only to be careful—and lucky—to live a long time in the Solomons; but he must also be of the right sort. He must have the hall-mark of the inevitable white man stamped upon his soul. He must be inevitable. He must have a certain grand carelessness of odds, a certain colossal self-satisfaction, and a racial egotism that convinces him that one white is better than a thousand niggers every day in the week, and that on Sunday he is able to clean out two thousand niggers. For such are the things that have made the white man inevitable. Oh, and one other thing —the white man who wishes to be inevitable, must not merely despise the lesser breeds and think a lot of himself; he must also fail to be too long on imagination. He must not understand too well the instincts, customs, and mental processes of the blacks, the yellows, and the browns; for it is not in such fashion that the white race has tramped its royal road around the world.

Bertie Arkwright was not inevitable. He was too sensitive, too finely strung, and he possessed too much imagination. The world was too much with him. He projected himself too quiveringly into his environment. Therefore, the last place in the world for him to come was the Solomons. He did not come expecting to stay. A five weeks' stop-over between steamers, he decided, would satisfy the call of the primitive he felt thrum-ming the strings of his being. At least, so he told the lady tourists on the *Makembo*, though in different terms; and they worshipped him as a hero, for they were lady tourists and they would know only the safety of the steamer's deck as she threaded her way through the Solomons.

There was another man on board, of whom the ladies took no notice. He was a little shrivelled wisp of a man, with a withered skin the colour of mahogany. His name on the passenger list does not matter but his other name, Captain Malu, was a name for niggers to conjure with, and to scare naughty pickaninnies to righteousness, from New Hanover to the New Hebrides. He had farmed savages and savagery, and from fever and hardship, the crack of Sniders and the lash of the overseers, had wrested five millions of money in the form of bêche-de-mer, sandal-wood, pearl-shell and turtle-shell, ivory-nuts and copra, grasslands, trading stations, and planta-tions. Captain Malu's little finger, which was broken, had more inevitableness in it than Bertie Arkwright's whole carcass. But then, the lady tourists had nothing by which to judge save appearances, and Bertie certainly was a fine-looking man.

Bertie talked with Captain Malu in the smoking-room, confiding to him his intention of seeing life red and bleeding in the Solomons. Captain Malu agreed that the intention was ambitious and honourable. It was not until several days later that he became interested in Bertie, when that young adventurer insisted on showing him an automatic 44-calibre pistol. Bertie explained the mechanism and demonstrated by slipping a loaded magazine up the hollow butt.

'It is so simple,' he said. He shot the outer barrel back along the inner one. 'That loads it and cocks it, you see. And then all I have to do is pull the trigger, eight times, as fast as I can quiver my finger. See that safety clutch. That's what I like about it. It is safe. It is positively fool-proof.' He slipped out the magazine. 'You see how safe it is.'

As he held it in his hand, the muzzle came in line with Captain Malu's stomach. Captain Malu's blue eyes looked at it unswervingly.

'Would you mind pointing it in some other direction?' he asked.

'It's perfectly safe,' Bertie assured him. 'I withdrew the magazine. It's not loaded now, you know.'

'A gun is always loaded.'

'But this one isn't.'

'Turn it away just the same.'

Captain Malu's voice was flat and metallic and low, but his eyes never left the muzzle until the line of it was drawn past him and away from him.

'I'll bet a fiver it isn't loaded,' Bertie proposed warmly.

The other shook his head.

'Then I'll show you.'

Bertie started to put the muzzle to his own temple with the evident intention of pulling the trigger.

'Just a second,' Captain Malu said quietly, reaching out his hand. 'Let me look at it.'

He pointed it seaward and pulled the trigger.

A heavy explosion followed, instantaneous with a sharp click of the mechanism that flipped a hot and smoking cartridge sidewise along the deck. Bertie's jaw dropped in amazement.

'I slipped the barrel back once, didn't I?' he explained. 'It was silly of me, I must say.'

He giggled flabbily, and sat down in a steamer chair. The blood had ebbed from his face, exposing dark circles under his eyes. His hands were trembling and unable to guide the shaking cigarette to his lips. The world was too much with him, and he saw himself with dripping brains prone upon the deck.

'Really,' he said, '. . . really.'

'It's a pretty weapon,' said Captain Malu, returning the automatic to him.

The Commissioner was on board the *Makembo*, returning from Sydney, and by his permission a stop was made at Ugi to land a missionary. And at Ugi lay the ketch *Arla*, Captain Hansen, skipper. Now the *Arla* was one of many vessels owned by Captain Malu, and it was at his suggestion and by his invitation that Bertie went aboard the *Arla* as guest for a four days' recruiting cruise on the coast of Malaita. Thereafter the *Arla* would drop him at Reminge Plantation (also owned by Captain Malu), where Bertie could remain for a week, and then be sent over to Tulagi, the seat of government, where he would become the Commissioner's guest. Captain Malu was responsible for two other suggestions, which given, he disappears from this narrative. One was to Captain Hansen, the other to Mr. Harriwell, manager of Reminge Plantation. Both suggestions were similar in tenor, namely, to give Mr. Bertram Arkwright an insight into the rawness and redness of life in the Solomons. Also, it is whispered that Captain Malu mentioned that a case of Scotch would be coincidental with any particularly gorgeous insight Mr. Arkwright might receive.

'Yes, Swartz always was too pig-headed. You see, he took four of his boat's crew to Tulgi to be flogged—officially, you know—then started back with them in the whale-boat. It was pretty squally, and the boat capsized just outside. Swartz was the only one drowned. Of course it was an accident.'

'Was it? Really?' Bertie asked, only half-interested, staring hard at the black man at the wheel.

Ugi had dropped astern, and the *Arla* was sliding along through a summer sea toward the wooded ranges of Malaita. The helmsman who so attracted Bertie's eyes sported a ten-penny nail, stuck skewer-wise through his nose. About his neck was a string of pants' buttons. Thrust through holes in his ears were a can-opener, the broken handle of a tooth-brush, a clay pipe, the brass wheel of an alarum clock, and several Winchester rifle cartridges. On his chest, suspended from around his neck, hung the half of a china plate. Some forty similarly apparelled blacks lay about the deck, fifteen of which were boat's crew, the remainder being fresh labour recruits.

'Of course it was an acccident,' spoke up the *Arla*'s mate,

Jacobs, a slender, dark-eyed man who looked more a professor than a sailor. 'Johnny Bedip nearly had the same kind of accident. He was bringing back several from a flogging, when they capsized him. But he knew how to swim as well as they, and two of them were drowned. He used a boat-stretcher and a revolver. Of course it was an accident.'

'Quite common, them accidents,' remarked the skipper. 'You see that man at the wheel, Mr. Arkwright? He's a man-eater. Six months ago, he and the rest of the boat's crew drowned the then captain of the *Arla*. They did it on deck, sir, right aft there by the mizzen-traveller.'

'The deck was in a shocking state,' said the mate.

'Do I understand——?' Bertie began.

'Yes, just that,' said Captain Hansen. 'It was accidental drowning.'

'But on deck—?'

'Just so. I don't mind telling you, in confidence, of course, that they used an axe.'

'This present crew of yours?'

Captain Hansen nodded.

'The other skipper always was too careless,' explained the mate. 'He but just turned his back, when they let him have it.'

'We haven't any show down here,' was the skipper's complaint. 'The Government protects a nigger against a white every time. You can't shoot first. You've got to give the nigger first shot, or else the Government calls it murder and you go to Fiji. That's why there's so many drowning accidents.'

Dinner was called, and Bertie and the skipper went below, leaving the mate to watch on deck.

'Keep an eye out for that black devil, Auiki,' was the skipper's parting caution. 'I haven't liked his looks for several days.'

'Righto,' said the mate.

Dinner was part way along, and the skipper was in the middle of his story of the cutting out of the *Scottish Chiefs*.

'Yes,' he was saying, 'she was the finest vessel on the coast. But when she missed stays, and before ever she hit the reef, the canoes started for her. There were five white men, a crew of twenty Santa Cruz boys and Samoans, and only the super-cargo escaped. Besides, there were sixty recruits. They were all *kai-kai'd*. *Kai-kai?*—oh, I beg your pardon. I mean they were eaten. Then there was the *James Edwards*, a dandy-rigged—'

But at that moment there was a sharp oath from the mate on deck and a chorus of savage cries. A revolver went off three times, and then was heard a loud splash. Captain Hansen had sprung up the companionway on the instant, and Bertie's eyes had been fascinated by a glimpse of him drawing his revolver as he sprang. Bertie went up more circumspectly, hesitating before he put his head above the companionway slide. But nothing happened. The mate was shaking with excitement, his revolver in his hand. Once he started, and half-jumped around, as if danger threatened his back.

'One of the natives fell overboard,' he was saying, in a queer tense voice. 'He couldn't swim.'

'Who was it?' the skipper demanded.

'Auiki,' was the answer.

'But I say, you know, I heard shots,' Bertie said, in trembling eagerness, for he scented adventure, and adventure that was happily over with.

The mate whirled upon him, snarling:

'It's a damned lie. There ain't been a shot fired. The nigger fell overboard.'

Captain Hansen regarded Bertie with unblinking, lacklustre eyes.

'I—I thought—' Bertie was beginning.

'Shots?' said Captain Hansen, dreamily. 'Shots? Did you hear any shots, Mr. Jacobs?'

'Not a shot,' replied Mr. Jacobs.

The skipper looked at his guest triumphantly, and said:

'Evidently an accident. Let us go down, Mr. Arkwright, and finish dinner.'

Bertie slept that night in the captain's cabin, a tiny stateroom off the main-cabin. The for'ard bulkhead was decorated with a stand of rifles. Over the bunk were three more rifles. Under the bunk was a big drawer, which, when he pulled it out, he found filled with ammunition, dynamite, and several boxes of detonators. He elected to take the settee on the opposite side. Lying conspicuously on the small table, was the *Arla*'s log. Bertie did not know that it had been especially prepared for the occasion by Captain Malu, and he read therein how on September 21, two boat's crew had fallen overboard and been drowned. Bertie read between the lines and knew better. He read how the *Arla*'s whale-boat had been bushwhacked at Su'u and had lost three men; of how the skipper discovered the cook stewing human flesh on the galley fire— flesh purchased by the boat's crew ashore in Fui; of how an accidental discharge of dynamite, while signalling, had killed another boat's crew; of night attacks; ports fled from between the dawns; attacks by bushmen in mangrove swamps and by fleets of salt-water men in the larger passages. One item that occurred with monotonous frequency was death by dysentery. He noticed with alarm that two white men had so died—guests, like himself, on the *Arla*.

'I say, you know,' Bertie said next day to Captain Hansen. 'I've been glancing through your log.'

The skipper displayed quick vexation that the log had been left lying about.

'And all that dysentery, you know, that's all rot, just like the accidental drownings,' Bertie continued. 'What does dysentery really stand for?'

The skipper openly admired his guest's acumen, stiffened himself to make indignant denial, then gracefully surrendered.

'You see, it's like this, Mr. Arkwright. These islands have got a bad enough name as it is. It's getting harder every day to sign on white men. Suppose a man is killed. The company has to pay through the nose for another man to take the job. But if the man merely dies of sickness, it's all right. The new chums don't mind disease. What they draw the line at is being murdered. I thought the skipper of the *Arla* had died of dysentery when I took his billet. Then it was too late. I'd signed the contract.'

'Besides,' said Mr. Jacobs, 'there's altogether too many accidental drownings anyway. It don't look right. It's the fault of the Government. A white man hasn't a chance to defend himself from the niggers.'

'Yes, look at the *Princess* and that Yankee mate,' the skipper took up the tale. 'She carried five white men besides a Government agent. The captain, the agent, and the super-cargo were ashore in the two boats. They were killed to the last man. The mate and bosun, with about fifteen of the crew—Samoans and Tongans—were on board. A crowd of niggers came off from shore. First thing the mate knew, the bosun and the crew were killed in the first rush. The mate grabbed three cartridge-belts and two Winchesters and skinned up to the cross-trees. He was the sole survivor, and you can't blame him for being mad. He pumped one rifle till it got so hot he couldn't hold it, then he pumped the other. The deck was black with niggers. He cleaned them out. He dropped them as they went over the rail, and he dropped them as fast as they picked up their paddles. Then they jumped into the water and started to swim for it, and, being mad, he got half a dozen more. And what did he get for it?'

'Seven years in Fiji,' snapped the mate.

'The Government said he wasn't justified in shooting after they'd taken to the water,' the skipper explained.

'And that's why they die of dysentery nowadays,' the mate added.

'Just fancy,' said Bertie, as he felt a longing for the cruise to be over.

Later on in the day he interviewed the black who had been pointed out to him as a cannibal. This fellow's name was Sumasai. He had spent three years on a Queensland plantation. He had been to Samoa, and Fiji, and Sydney; and as a boat's crew had been on recruiting schooners through New Britain, New Ireland, New Guinea, and the Admiralties. Also, he was a wag, and he had taken a line on his skipper's conduct. Yes, he had eaten many men. How many? He could not remember the tally. Yes, white men, too; they were very good, unless they were sick. He had once eaten a sick one.

'My word!' he cried, at the recollection. 'Me sick plenty along him. My belly walk about too much.'

Bertie shuddered, and asked about heads. Yes, Sumasai had several hidden ashore, in good condition, sun-dried, and smoke-cured. One was of the captain of a schooner. It had long whiskers. He would sell it for two quid. Black men's heads he would sell for one quid. He had some pickaninny heads in poor condition, that he would let go for ten bob.

Five minutes afterward, Bertie found himself sitting on the companionway-slide alongside a black with a horrible skin disease. He sheered off, and on inquiry was told that it was leprosy. He hurried below and washed himself with antiseptic soap. He took many antiseptic washes in the course of the day, for every native on board was afflicted with malignant ulcers of one sort or another.

As the *Arla* drew in to an anchorage in the midst of mangrove swamps, a double row of barbed wire stretched around above her rail. That looked like business, and when Bertie saw the shore canoes alongside, armed with spears, bows and arrows, and Sniders, he wished more earnestly than ever that the cruise was over.

That evening the natives were slow in leaving the ship at sundown. A number of them cheeked the mate when he ordered them ashore.

'Never mind, I'll fix them,' said Captain Hansen, diving below.

When he came back, he showed Bertie a stick of dynamite attached to a fish-hook. Now it happens that a paper-wrapped bottle of chlorodyne with a piece of harmless fuse projecting can fool anybody. It fooled Bertie, and it fooled the natives. When Captain Hansen lighted the fuse and hooked the fish-hook into the tail end of a native's loin-cloth, that native was smitten with so ardent a desire for the shore that he forgot to shed the loin-cloth. He started for'ard, the fuse sizzling and spluttering at his rear, the natives in his path taking headers over the barbed wire at every jump. Bertie was horror-stricken. So was Captain Hansen. He had forgotten his twenty-five recruits, on each of which he had paid thirty shillings advance. They went over the side along with the shore-dwelling folk and followed by him who trailed the sizzling chlorodyne bottle.

Bertie did not see the bottle go off; but the mate opportunely discharging a stick of real dynamite aft where it would harm nobody, Bertie would have sworn in any admiralty court to a nigger blown to flinders.

The flight of the twenty-five recruits had actually cost the *Arla* forty pounds, and, since they had taken to the bush, there was no hope of recovering them. The skipper and his mate proceeded to drown their sorrow in cold tea. The cold tea was in whisky bottles, so Bertie did not know it was cold tea they were mopping up. All he knew was that the two men got very drunk and argued eloquently and at length as to whether the exploded nigger should be reported as a case of dysentery or as an accidental drowning. When they snored off to sleep, he was the only white man left, and he kept a perilous watch till dawn, in fear of an attack from shore and an uprising of the crew.

Three more days the *Arla* spent on the coast, and three more nights the skipper and the mate drank overfondly of cold tea, leaving Bertie to keep the watch. They knew he could be depended upon, he would report their drunken conduct to Captain Malu. Then the *Arla* dropped anchor at Reminge Plantation, on Guadalcanar, and Bertie landed on the beach with a sigh of relief and shook hands with the manager. Mr. Harriwell was ready for him.

'Now you mustn't be alarmed if some of our fellows seem downcast,' Mr. Harriwell said, having drawn him aside in confidence. 'There's been talk of an outbreak, and two or three suspicious signs I'm willing to admit, but personally I think it's all poppycock.'

'How—how many blacks have you on the plantation?' Bertie asked, with a sinking heart.

'We're working four hundred just now,' replied Mr. Harriwell, cheerfully; 'but the three of us, with you, of course, and the skipper and mate of the *Arla*, can handle them all right.'

Bertie turned to meet one McTavish, the storekeeper, who scarcely acknowledged the introduction, such was his eagerness to present his resignation.

'It being that I'm a married man, Mr. Harriwell, I can't very well afford to remain on longer. Trouble is working up, as plain as the nose on your face. The niggers are going to break out, and there'll be another Hohono horror here.'

'What's a Hohono horror?' Bertie asked, after the storekeeper had been persuaded to remain until the end of the month.

'Oh, he means Hohono Plantation, on Ysabel,' said the manager. 'The niggers killed the five white men ashore, captured the schooner, killed the captain and mate, and escaped in a body to Malaita. But I always said they were careless on Hohono. They won't catch us napping here. Come along, Mr. Arkwright, and see our view from the verandah.'

Bertie was too busy wondering how he could get away to Tulagi to the Commissioner's house, to see much of the view. He was still wondering, when a rifle exploded very near him, behind his back. At the same moment his arm was nearly dislocated, so eagerly did Mr. Harriwell drag him indoors.

'I say, old man, that was a close shave,' said the manager, pawing him over to see if he had been hit. 'I can't tell you how sorry I am. But it was broad daylight, and I never dreamed.'

Bertie was beginning to turn pale.

'They got the other manager that way,' McTavish vouchsafed. 'And a dashed fine chap he was. Blew his brains out all over the verandah. You noticed that dark stain there between the steps and the door?'

Bertie was ripe for the cocktail which Mr. Harriwell pitched in and compounded for him; but before he could drink it, a man in riding trousers and putties entered.

'What's the matter now?' the manager asked, after one look at the newcomer's face. 'Is the river up again?'

'River be blowed—it's the niggers. Stepped out of the canegrass, not a dozen feet away, and whopped at me. It was a

Snider, and he shot from the hip. Now what I want to know is where'd he get that Snider?—Oh, I beg pardon. Glad to know you, Mr. Arkwright.'

'Mr. Brown is my assistant,' explained Mr. Harriwell. 'And now let's have that drink.'

'But where'd he get that Snider?' Mr. Brown insisted. 'I always objected to keeping those guns on the premises.'

'They're still there,' Mr. Harriwell said, with a show of heat.

Mr. Brown smiled incredulously.

'Come along and see,' said the manager.

Bertie joined the procession into the office, where Mr. Harriwell pointed triumphantly at a big packing-case in a dusty corner.

'Well, then, where did the beggar get that Snider?' harped Mr. Brown.

But just then McTavish lifted the packing-case. The manager started, then tore off the lid. The case was empty. They gazed at one another in horrified silence. Harriwell drooped wearily.

Then McTavish cursed.

'What I contended all along—the house-boys are not to be trusted.'

'It does look serious,' Harriwell admitted, 'but we'll come through it all right. What the sanguinary niggers need is a shaking up. Will you gentlemen please bring your rifles to dinner, and will you, Mr. Brown, kindly prepare forty or fifty sticks of dynamite. Make the fuses good and short. We'll give them a lesson. And now, gentlemen, dinner is served.'

One thing that Bertie detested was rice and curry, so it happened that he alone partook of an inviting omelet. He had quite finished his plate, when Harriwell helped himself to the omelet. One mouthful he tasted, then spat out vociferously.

'That's the second time,' McTavish announced ominously.

Harriwell was still hawking and spitting.

'Second time, what?' Bertie quavered.

'Poison,' was the answer. 'That cook will be hanged yet.'

'That's the way the book-keeper went out at Cape Marsh,' Brown spoke up. 'Died horribly. They said on the *Jessie* that they heard him screaming three miles away.'

'I'll put the cook in irons,' sputtered Harriwell. 'Fortunately we discovered it in time.'

Bertie sat paralysed. There was no colour in his face. He attempted to speak, but only an inarticulate gurgle resulted. All eyed him anxiously.

'Don't say it, don't say it,' McTavish cried in a tense voice.

'Yes, I ate it, plenty of it, a whole plateful!' Bertie cried explosively, like a diver suddenly regaining breath.

The awful silence continued half a minute longer, and he read his fate in their eyes.

'Maybe it wasn't poison after all,' said Harriwell, dismally.

'Call in the cook,' said Brown.

In came the cook, a grinning black boy, nose-spiked and ear-plugged.

'Here you, Wi-wi, what name that?' Harriwell bellowed, pointing accusingly at the omelet.

Wi-wi was very naturally frightened and embarrassed.

'Him good fella *kai-kai*,' he murmured apologetically.

'Make him eat it,' suggested McTavish. 'That's the proper test.'

Harriwell filled a spoon with the stuff and jumped for the cook, who fled in panic.

'That settles it,' was Brown's solemn pronouncement. 'He won't eat it.'

'Mr. Brown, will you please go and put the irons on him?' Harriwell turned cheerfully to Bertie. 'It's all right, old man, the Commissioner will deal with him, and if you die, depend upon it, he will be hanged.'

'Don't think the Government'll do it,' objected McTavish.

'But, gentlemen, gentlemen,' Bertie cried. 'In the meantime think of me.'

Harriwell shrugged his shoulders pityingly.

'Sorry, old man, but it's a native poison, and there are no known antidotes for native poisons. Try and compose yourself, and if—'

Two sharp reports of a rifle from without interrupted the discourse, and Brown, entering, reloaded his rifle and sat down to table.

'The cook's dead,' he said. 'Fever. A rather sudden attack.'

'I was just telling Mr. Arkwright that there are no antidotes for native poisons—'

'Except gin,' said Brown.

Harriwell called himself an absent-minded idiot and rushed for the gin bottle.

'Neat, man, neat,' he warned Bertie, who gulped down a tumbler two-thirds full of the raw spirits, and coughed and choked from the angry bite of it till the tears ran down his cheeks.

Harriwell took his pulse and temperature, made a show of

looking out for him, and doubted that the omelet had been poisoned. Brown and McTavish also doubted; but Bertie discerned an insincere ring in their voices. His appetite had left him, and he took his own pulse stealthily under the table. There was no question but what it was increasing, but he failed to ascribe it to the gin he had taken. McTavish, rifle in hand, went out on the verandah to reconnoitre.

'They're massing up at the cook-house,' was his report. 'And they've no end of Sniders. My idea is to sneak around on the other side and take them in flank. Strike the first blow, you know. Will you come along, Brown?'

Harriwell ate on steadily, while Bertie discovered that his pulse had leaped up five beats. Nevertheless, he could not help jumping when the rifles began to go off. Above the scattering of Sniders could be heard the pumping of Brown's and McTavish's Winchesters—all against a background of demoniacal screeching and yelling.

'They've got them on the run,' Harriwell remarked, as voices and gunshots faded away in the distance.

Scarcely were Brown and McTavish back at the table when the latter reconnoitred.

'They've got dynamite,' he said.

'Then let's charge them with dynamite,' Harriwell proposed.

Thrusting half a dozen sticks each into their pockets and equipping themselves with lighted cigars, they started for the door. And just then it happened. They blamed McTavish for it afterwards, and he admitted that the charge had been a trifle excessive. But at any rate it went off under the house, which lifted up corner wise and settled back on its foundations. Half the china on the table was shattered, while the eight-day clock stopped. Yelling for vengeance, the three men rushed out into the night, and the bombardment began.

When they returned, there was no Bertie. He had dragged himself away to the office, barricaded himself in, and sunk upon the floor in a gin-soaked nightmare, wherein he died a thousand deaths while the valorous fight went on around him. In the morning, sick and headachey from the gin, he crawled out to find the sun still in the sky and God presumably in heaven, for his hosts were alive and uninjured.

Harriwell pressed him to stay on longer, but Bertie insisted on sailing immediately on the *Arla* for Tulagi, where, until the following steamer day, he stuck close by the Commissioner's house. There were lady tourists on the outgoing steamer, and Bertie was again a hero, while Captain Malu, as usual, passed unnoticed. But Captain Malu sent back from Sydney two cases of the best Scotch whisky on the market, for he was not able to make up his mind as to whether it was Captain Hansen or Mr. Harriwell who had given Bertie Arkwright the more gorgeous insight into life in the Solomons.

The Unparalleled
Invasion

It was in the year 1976 that the trouble between the world and China reached its culmination. It was because of this that the celebration of the Second Centennial of American Liberty was deferred. Many other plans of the nations of the earth were twisted and tangled and postponed for the same reason. The world awoke rather abruptly to its danger; but for over seventy years, unperceived, affairs had been shaping towards this very end.

The year 1904 logically marks the beginning of the development that, seventy years later, was to bring consternation to the whole world. The Japanese-Russian War took place in 1904, and the historians of the time gravely noted it down that that event marked the entrance of Japan into the comity of nations. What it really did mark was the awakening of China. This awakening, long expected, had finally been given up. The Western nations had tried to arouse China, and they had failed. Out of their native optimism and race-egoism they had therefore concluded that the task was impossible, that China would never awaken.

What they had failed to take into account was this: *that between them and China was no common psychological speech.* Their thought-processes were radically dissimilar. There was no intimate vocabulary. The Western mind penetrated the Chinese mind but a short distance when it found itself in a fathomless maze. The Chinese mind penetrated the Western mind an equally short distance when it fetched up against a blank, incomprehensible wall. It was all a matter of language. There was no way to communicate Western ideas to the Chinese mind. China remained asleep. The material achievement and progress of the West was a closed book to her; nor could the West open the book. Back and deep down on the tie-ribs of consciousness, in the mind, say, of the English-speaking race, was a capacity to thrill to short, Saxon words; back and deep down on the tie-ribs of consciousness of the Chinese mind was a capacity to thrill to its own hieroglyphics; but the Chinese mind could not thrill to short, Saxon words; nor could the English-speaking mind thrill to hieroglyphics. The fabrics of their minds were woven from totally different stuffs. They were mental aliens. And so it was the Western material achievement and progress made no dent on the rounded sleep of China.

Came Japan and her victory over Russia in 1904. Now the Japanese race was the freak and paradox among Eastern peoples. In some strange way Japan was receptive to all the West had to offer. Japan so swiftly assimilated Western ideas, and digested them, and so capably applied them that she suddenly burst forth, full-panoplied, a world-power. There is no explaining this peculiar openness of Japan to the alien culture of the West. As well might be explained any biological sport in the animal kingdom.

Having decisively thrashed the great Russian Empire, Japan promptly set about dreaming a colossal dream of empire for herself. Korea she had made into a granary and a colony; treaty privileges and vulpine diplomacy gave her the monopoly of Manchuria. But Japan was not satisfied. She turned her eyes upon China. There lay a vast territory, and in that territory were the hugest deposits in the world of iron and coal—the backbone of industrial civilization. Given natural resources, the other great factor in industry is labour. In that territory was a population of 400,000,000 souls—one quarter of the then total population of the earth. Furthermore, the Chinese were excellent workers, while their fatalistic philosophy (or religion) and their stolid nervous organization constituted them splendid soldiers—if they were properly managed. Needless to say, Japan was prepared to furnish that management.

But best of all, from the standpoint of Japan, the Chinese was a kindred race. The baffling enigma of the Chinese character to the West was no baffling enigma to the Japanese. The Japanese understood as we could never school ourselves

or hope to understand. Their mental processes were the same.
The Japanese thought with the same thought-symbols as did
the Chinese, and they thought in the same peculiar grooves.
Into the Chinese mind the Japanese went on where we were
baulked by the obstacle of incomprehension. They took the
turning which we could not perceive, twisted around the
obstacle, and were out of sight in the ramifications of the
Chinese mind where we could not follow. They were brothers.
Long ago one had borrowed the other's written language, and,
untold generations before that, they had diverged from the
common Mongol stock. There had been changes, differen-
tiations brought about by diverse conditions and infusions of
other blood; but down at the bottom of the beings, twisted
into the fibres of them, was a heritage in common, a sameness
in kind that time had not obliterated.

And so Japan took upon herself the management of China.
In the years immediately following the war with Russia, her
agents swarmed over the Chinese Empire. A thousand miles
beyond the last mission station toiled her engineers and spies,
clad as coolies, under the guise of itinerant merchants or
proselytizing Buddhist priests, noting down the horse-power
of every waterfall, the likely sites for factories, the heights of
mountains and passes, the strategic advantages and weak-
nesses, the wealth of the farming valleys, the number of
bullocks in a district or the number of labourers that could be
collected by forced levies. Never was there such a census, and
it could have been taken by no other people than the dogged,
patient, patriotic Japanese.

But in a short time secrecy was thrown to the winds.
Japan's officers reorganized the Chinese army; her drill
sergeants made the medieval warriors over into twentieth-
century soldiers, accustomed to all the modern machinery of
war and with a higher average of marksmanship than the
soldiers of any Western nation. The engineers of Japan deep-
ened and widened the intricate system of canals, built factories
and foundries, netted the empire with telegraphs and tele-
phones, and inaugurated the era of railroad-building. It was
these same protagonists of machine-civilization that discovered
the great oil deposits of Chunsan, the iron mountains of
Whang-Sing, the copper ranges of Chinchi, and they sank the
gas wells of Wow-Wee, that most marvellous reservoir of
natural gas in all the world.

In China's councils of empire were the Japanese emissaries.
In the ears of the statesmen whispered the Japanese statesmen.

The political reconstruction of the Empire was due to them. They evicted the scholar class, which was violently reactionary, and put into office progressive officials. And in every town and city of the Empire newspapers were started. Of course, Japanese editors ran the policy of these papers, which policy they got direct from Tokio. It was these papers that educated and made progressive the great mass of the population.

China was at last awake. Where the West had failed, Japan succeeded. She had transmuted Western culture and achievement into terms that were intelligible to the Chinese understanding. Japan herself, when she so suddenly awakened, had astounded the world. But at the time she was only forty millions strong. China's awakening, with her four hundred millions and the scientific advance of the world, was frightfully astounding. She was the colossus of the nations, and swiftly her voice was heard in no uncertain tones in the affairs and councils of the nations. Japan egged her on, and the proud Western peoples listened with respectful ears.

China's swift and remarkable rise was due, perhaps more than to anything else, to the superlative quality of her labour. The Chinese was the perfect type of industry. He had always been that. For sheer ability to work no worker in the world could compare with him. Work was the breath of his nostrils. It was to him what wandering and fighting in far lands and spiritual adventure had been to other peoples. Liberty, to him, epitomized itself in access to the means of toil. To till the soil and labour interminably was all he asked of life and the powers that be. And the awakening of China had given its vast population not merely free and unlimited access to the means of toil, but access to the highest and most scientific machine-means of toil.

China rejuvenescent! It was but a step to China rampant. She discovered a new pride in herself and a will of her own. She began to chafe under the guidance of Japan, but she did not chafe long. On Japan's advice, in the beginning, she had expelled from the Empire all Western missionaries, engineers, drill sergeants, merchants, and teachers. She now began to expel the similar representatives of Japan. The latter's advisory statesmen were showered with honours and decorations, and sent home. The West had awakened Japan, and, as Japan had then requited the West, Japan was now requited by China. Japan was thanked for her kindly aid and flung out bag and baggage by her gigantic protégé. The Western nations chuckled. Japan's rainbow dream had gone glimmering. She grew angry.

China laughed at her. The blood and the swords of the Samurai would out, and Japan rashly went to war. This occurred in 1922, and in seven bloody months Manchuria, Korea, and Formosa were taken away from her and she was hurled back, bankrupt, to stifle in her tiny, crowded islands. Exit Japan from the world drama. Thereafter she devoted herself to art, and her task became to please the world greatly with her creations of wonder and beauty.

Contrary to expectation, China did not prove warlike. She had no Napoleonic dream, and was content to devote herself to the arts of peace. After a time of disquiet, the idea was accepted that China was to be feared, not in war, but in commerce. It will be seen that the real danger was not apprehended. China went on consummating her machine-civilization. Instead of a large standing army, she developed an immensely larger and splendidly efficient militia. Her navy was so small that it was the laughing-stock of the world; nor did she attempt to strengthen her navy. The treaty ports of the world were never entered by her visiting battleships.

The real danger lay in the fecundity of her loins, and it was in 1970 that the first cry of alarm was raised. For some time all territories adjacent to China had been grumbling at Chinese immigration; but now it suddenly came home to the world that China's population was 500,000,000. She had increased by a hundred millions since her awakening. Burchaldter called attention to the fact that there were more Chinese in existence than white-skinned people. He performed a simple sum in arithmetic. He added together the populations of the United States, Canada, New Zealand, Australia, South Africa, England, France, Germany, Italy, Austria, European Russia, and all Scandinavia. The result was 495,000,000. And the population of China overtopped this tremendous total by 5,000,000. Burchaldter's figures went round the world, and the world shivered.

For many centuries China's population had been constant. Her territory had been saturated with population; that is to say, her territory, with the primitive method of production, had supported the maximum limit of population. But when she awoke and inaugurated the machine-civilization, her productive power had been enormously increased. Thus, on the same territory, she was able to support a far larger population. At once the birth rate began to rise and the death rate to fall. Before, when population pressed against the means of subsistence, the excess population had been swept away by famine. But now, thanks to the machine-civilization, China's means of subsistence had been enormously extended, and there were no famines; her population followed on the heels of the increase in the means of subsistence.

During this time of transition and development of power, China had entertained no dreams of conquest. The Chinese was not an imperial race. It was industrious, thrifty, and peace-loving. War was looked upon as an unpleasant but necessary task that at times must be performed. And so, while the Western races had squabbled and fought, and world-adventured against one another, China had calmly gone on working at her machines and growing. Now she was spilling over the boundaries of her Empire—that was all, just spilling over into the adjacent territories with all the certainty and terrifying slow momentum of a glacier.

Following upon the alarm raised by Burchaldter's figures, in 1970, France made a long-threatened stand. French Indo-China had been overrun, filled up, by Chinese immigrants. France called a halt. The Chinese wave flowed on. France assembled a force of a hundred thousand on the boundary between her unfortunate colony and China, and China sent down an army of militia-soldiers a million strong. Behind came the wives and sons and daughters and relatives, with their personal household luggage, in a second army. The French force was brushed aside like a fly. The Chinese militia-soldiers, along with their families, over five millions all told, coolly took possession of French Indo-China and settled down to stay for a few thousand years.

Outraged France was in arms. She hurled fleet after fleet against the coast of China, and nearly bankrupted herself by the effort. China had no navy. She withdrew like a turtle into her shell. For a year the French fleets blockaded the coast and bombarded exposed towns and villages. China did not mind. She did not depend upon the rest of the world for anything. She calmly kept out of range of the French guns and went on working. France wept and wailed, wrung her impotent hands and appealed to the dumbfounded nations. Then she landed a punitive expedition to march to Peking. It was two hundred and fifty thousand strong, and it was the flower of France. It landed without opposition and marched into the interior. And that was the last ever seen of it. The line of communication was snapped on the second day. Not a survivor came back to tell what had happened. It had been swallowed up in China's cavernous maw, that was all.

In the five years that followed, China's expansion, in all land directions, went on apace. Siam was made part of the Empire, and, in spite of all that England could do, Burma and the Malay Peninsula were overrun; while all along the long south boundary of Siberia, Russia was pressed severely by China's advancing hordes. The process was simple. First came the Chinese immigration (or, rather, it was already there, having come there slowly and insidiously during the previous years). Next came the clash of arms and the brushing away of all opposition by a monster army of militia-soldiers, followed by their families and household baggage. And finally came their settling down as colonists in the conquered territory. Never was there so strange and effective a method of world conquest.

Nepal and Bhutan were overrun, and the whole northern boundary of India pressed against by this fearful tide of life. To the west, Bokhara, and, even to the south and west, Afghanistan, were swallowed up. Persia, Turkestan, and all Central Asia felt the pressure of the flood. It was at this time that Burchaldter revised his figures. He had been mistaken. China's population must be seven hundred millions, eight hundred millions, nobody knew how many millions, but at any rate it would soon be a billion. There were two Chinese for every white-skinned human in the world, Burchaldter announced, and the world trembled. China's increase must have begun immediately, in 1904. It was remembered that since that date there had not been a single famine. At 5,000,000 a year increase, her total increase in the intervening seventy years must be 350,000,000. But who was to know? It might be more. Who was to know anything of this strange new menace of the twentieth century—China, old China, rejuvenescent, fruitful, and militant!

The Convention of 1975 was called at Philadelphia. All the Western nations, and some few of the Eastern, were represented. Nothing was accomplished. There was talk of all countries putting bounties on children to increase the birth rate, but it was laughed to scorn by the arithmeticians, who pointed out that China was too far in the lead in that direction. No feasible way of coping with China was suggested. China was appealed to and threatened by the United Powers, and that was all the Convention of Philadelphia came to; and the Convention and the Powers were laughed at by China. Li Tang Fwung, the power behind the Dragon Throne, deigned to reply.

'What does China care for the comity of nations?' said Li

Tang Fwung. 'We are the most ancient, honourable, and royal of races. We have our own destiny to accomplish. It is unpleasant that our destiny does not tally with the destiny of the rest of the world, but what would you? You have talked windily about the royal races and the heritage of the earth, and we can only reply that that remains to be seen. You cannot invade us. Never mind about your navies. Don't shout. We know our navy is small. You see, we use it for police purposes. We do not care for the sea. Our strength is in our population, which will soon be a billion. Thanks to you, we are equipped with all modern war-machinery. Send your navies. We will not notice them. Send your punitive expeditions, but first remember France. To land half a million soldiers on our shores would strain the resources of any of you. And our thousand millions would swallow them down in a mouthful. Send a million; send five millions, and we will swallow them down just as readily. Pouf! A mere nothing, a meagre morsel. Destroy, as you have threatened, you United States, the ten million coolies we have forced upon your shoes—why, the amount scarcely equals half of our excess birth rate for a year.'

So spoke Li Tang Fwung. The world was nonplussed, helpless, terrified. Truly had he spoken. There was no combating China's amazing birth rate. If her population was a billion, and was increasing twenty millions a year, in twenty-five years it would be a billion and a half—equal to the total population of the world in 1904. And nothing could be done. There was no way to dam up the over-spilling monstrous flood of life. War was futile. China laughed at a blockade of her coasts. She welcomed invasion. In her capacious maw was room for all the hosts of earth that could be hurled at her. And in the meantime her flood of yellow life poured out and on over Asia. China laughed and read in their magazines the learned lucubrations of the distracted Western scholars.

But there was one scholar China failed to reckon on—Jacobus Laningdale. Not that he was a scholar, except in the widest sense. Primarily, Jacobus Laningdale was a scientist, and, up to that time, a very obscure scientist, a professor employed in the laboratories of the Health Office of New York City. Jacobus Laningdale's head was very like any other head, but in that head was evolved an idea. Also, in that head was the wisdom to keep that idea secret. He did not write an article for the magazines. Instead, he asked for a vacation. On September 19, 1975, he arrived in Washington. It was evening, but he proceeded straight to the White House, for he had already arranged an audience with the President. He was closeted with President Moyer for three hours. What passed between them was not learned by the rest of the world until long after; in fact, at that time the world was not interested in Jacobus Laningdale. Next day the President called in his Cabinet. Jacobus Laningdale was present. The proceedings were kept secret. But that very afternoon Rufus Cowdery, Secretary of State, left Washington, and early the following morning sailed for England. The secret that he carried began to spread, but it spread only among the heads of Governments. Possibly half-a-dozen men in a nation were entrusted with the idea that had formed in Jacobus Laningdale's head. Following the spread of the secret, sprang up great activity in all the dockyards, arsenals, and navy-yards. The people of France and Austria became suspicious, but so sincere were their Governments' calls for confidence that they acquiesced in the unknown project that was afoot.

This was the time of the Great Truce. All countries pledged themselves solemnly not to go to war with any other country. The first definite action was the gradual mobilization of the armies of Russia, Germany, Austria, Italy, Greece, and Turkey. Then began the eastward movement. All railroads into Asia were glutted with troop trains. China was the objective, that was all that was known. A little later began the great sea movement. Expeditions of warships were launched from all countries. Fleet followed fleet, and all proceeded to the coast of China. The nations cleaned out their navy-yards. They sent their revenue cutters and dispatch boats and lighthouse tenders, and they sent their last antiquated cruisers and battleships. Not content with this, they impressed the merchant marine. The statistics show that 58,640 merchant steamers, equipped with searchlights and rapid-fire guns, were dispatched by the various nations to China.

And China smiled and waited. On her land side, along her boundaries, were millions of the warriors of Europe. She mobilized five times as many millions of her militia and awaited the invasion. On her sea coasts she did the same. But China was puzzled. After all this enormous preparation, there was no invasion. She could not understand. Along the great Siberian frontier all was quiet. Along her coasts the towns and villages were not even shelled. Never, in the history of the world, had there been so mighty a gathering of war fleets. The fleets of all the world were there, and day and night millions of tons of battleships ploughed the brine of her coasts, and nothing happened. Nothing was attempted. Did they think to make her emerge from her shell? China smiled. Did they think to tire her out, or starve her out? China smiled again.

But on May 1, 1976, had the reader been in the imperial city of Peking, with its then population of eleven millions, he would have witnessed a curious sight. He would have seen the streets filled with the chattering yellow populace, every queued head tilted back, every slant eye turned skyward. And high up in the blue he would have beheld a tiny dot of black which, because of its orderly evolutions, he would have identified as an airship. From this airship, as it curved its flight back and forth over the city, fell missiles—strange, harmless missiles, tubes of fragile glass that shattered into thousands of fragments on the streets and house-tops. But there was nothing deadly about these tubes of glass. Nothing happened. There were no explosions. It is true, three Chinese were killed by the tubes dropping on their heads from so enormous a height; but what were three Chinese against an excess birth rate of twenty millions? One tube struck perpendicularly in a fish-pond in a garden and was not broken. It was dragged ashore by the master of the house. He did not dare to open it, but, accompanied by his friends, and surrounded by an ever-increasing crowd, he carried the mysterious tube to the magistrate of the district. The latter was a brave man. With all eyes upon him, he shattered the tube with a blow from his brass-bowled pipe. Nothing happened. Of those who were very near, one or two thought they saw some mosquitoes fly out. That was all. The crowd set up a great laugh and dispersed.

As Peking was bombarded by glass tubes, so was all China. The tiny airships, dispatched from the warships, contained but two men each, and over all cities, towns, and villages they wheeled and curved, one man directing the ship, the other man throwing over the glass tubes.

Had the reader again been in Peking, six weeks later, he would have looked in vain for the eleven million inhabitants. Some few of them he would have found, a few hundred thousand, perhaps, their carcases festering in the houses and in the deserted streets, and piled high on the abandoned death-wagons. But for the rest he would have had to seek along the highways and by-ways of the Empire. And not all would he have found fleeing from plague-stricken Peking, for behind them, by hundreds of thousands of unburied corpses by the wayside, he could have marked their flight. And as it was with Peking, so it was with all the cities, towns, and villages of the

Empire. The plague smote them all. Nor was it one plague, nor two plagues; it was a score of plagues. Every virulent form of infectious death stalked through the land. Too late the Chinese Government apprehended the meaning of the colossal preparations, the marshalling of the world-hosts, the flights of the tiny airships, and the rain of the tubes of glass. The proclamations of the Government were vain. They could not stop the eleven million plague-stricken wretches, fleeing from the one city of Peking to spread disease through all the land. The physicians and health officers died at their posts; and death, the all-conqueror, rode over the decrees of the Emperor and Li Tang Fwung. It rode over them as well, for Li Tang Fwung died in the second week, and the Emperor, hidden away in the Summer Palace, died in the fourth week.

Had there been one plague, China might have coped with it. But from a score of plagues no creature was immune. The man who escaped small pox went down before scarlet fever. The man who was immune to yellow fever was carried away by cholera; and if he were immune to that, too, the Black Death, which was the bubonic plague, swept him away. For it was these bacteria, and germs, and microbes, and bacilli, cultured in the laboratories of the West, that had come down upon China in the rain of glass.

All organization vanished. The government crumbled away. Decrees and proclamations were useless when the men who made them and signed them one moment were dead the next. Nor could the maddened millions, spurred on to flight by death, pause to heed anything. They fled from the cities to infect the country, and wherever they fled they carried the plagues with them. The hot summer was on—Jacobus Laningdale had selected the time shrewdly—and the plague festered everywhere. Much is conjectured of what occurred, and much has been learned from the stories of the few survivors. The wretched creatures stormed across the Empire in many-millioned flight. The vast armies China had collected on her frontiers melted away. The farms were ravaged for food, and no more crops were planted, while the crops already in were left unattended and never came to harvest. The most remarkable thing, perhaps, was the flights. Many millions engaged in them, charging to the bounds of the Empire to be met and turned back by the gigantic armies of the West. The slaughter of the mad hosts on the boundaries was stupendous. Time and again the guarding line was drawn back twenty or thirty miles to escape the contagion of the multitudinous dead.

Once the plague broke through and seized upon the German and Austrian soldiers who were guarding the borders of Turkestan. Preparations had been made for such a happening, and though sixty thousand soldiers of Europe were carried off, the international corps of physicians isolated the contagion and dammed it back. It was during this struggle that it was suggested that a new plague-germ had originated, that in some way or other a sort of hybridization between plague-germs had taken place, producing a new and frightfully virulent germ. First suspected by Vomberg, who became infected with it and died, it was later isolated and studied by Stevens, Hazenfelt, Norman, and Landers.

Such was the unparalleled invasion of China. For that billion of people there was no hope. Pent in their vast and festering charnel-house, all organization and cohesion lost, they could do naught but die. They could not escape. As they were flung back from their land frontiers, so were they flung back from the sea. Seventy-five thousand vessels patrolled the coasts. By day their smoking funnels dimmed the sea-rim, and by night their flashing searchlights ploughed the dark and harrowed it for the tiniest escaping junk. The attempts of the immense fleets of junks were pitiful. Not one ever got by the guarding sea-hounds. Modern war-machinery held back the disorganized mass of China, while the plagues did the work.

But old War was made a thing of laughter. Naught remained to him but patrol duty. China had laughed at war, and war she was getting, but it was ultra-modern war, twentieth-century war, the war of the scientist and the laboratory, the war of Jacobus Laningdale. Hundred-ton guns were toys compared with the micro-organic projectiles hurled from the laboratories, the messengers of death, the destroying angels that stalked through the empire of a billion souls.

During all the summer and fall of 1976 China was an inferno. There was no eluding the microscopic projectiles that sought out the remotest hiding-places. The hundreds of millions of dead remained unburied and the germs multiplied themselves, and, towards the last, millions died daily of starvation. Besides, starvation weakened the victims and destroyed their natural defences against the plagues. Cannibalism, murder, and madness reigned. And so perished China.

Not until the following February, in the coldest weather, were the first expeditions made. These expeditions were small, composed of scientists and bodies of troops; but they entered China from every side. In spite of the most elaborate precautions against infection, numbers of soldiers and a few of the physicians were stricken. But the exploration went bravely on. They found China devastated, a howling wilderness through which wandered bands of wild dogs and desperate bandits who had survived. All survivors were put to death wherever found. And then began the great task, the sanitation of China. Five years and hundreds of millions of treasure were consumed and then the world moved in—not in zones, as was the idea of Baron Albrecht, but heterogeneously, according to the democratic American programme. It was a vast and happy intermingling of nationalities that settled down in China in 1982 and the years that followed—a tremendous and successful experiment in cross-fertilization. We know today the splendid mechanical, intellectual, and art output that followed.

It was in 1987, the Great Truce having been dissolved, that the ancient quarrel between France and Germany over Alsace-Lorraine recrudesced. The war-cloud grew dark and threatening in April, and on April 17 the Convention of Copenhagen was called. The representatives of the nations of the world being present, all nations solemnly pledged themselves never to use against one another the laboratory methods of warfare they had employed in the invasion of China.